PENGUIN BOOKS

RITUALS

Cees Nooteboom is the author of novels, poetry collections, and travel books. He has been awarded several prizes during his career, including, in 1957, Second Prize from the Anne Frank Foundation for his critically acclaimed first novel *Philip en de anderen* (*Philip and the Others*) and, in 1963, the Van der Hootg Prize for his novel *De redder's gestorven* (*The Knight Has Fallen*). *Rituals* is the first of his books to be translated into English.

The Pegasus Prize for Literature

RITUALS

A NOVEL BY CEES NOOTEBOOM

Translated by Adrienne Dixon

PENGUIN BOOKS

PENGUIN BOOKS
Published by the Penguin Group
Viking Penguin, a division of Penguin Books USA Inc.,
375 Hudson Street, New York, New York 10014, U.S.A.
Penguin Books Ltd, 27 Wrights Lane,
London W8 5TZ, England
Penguin Books Australia Ltd, Ringwood,
Victoria, Australia
Penguin Books Canada Ltd, 10 Alcorn Avenue, Suite 300,
Toronto, Ontario, Canada M4V 3B2
Penguin Books (N.Z.) Ltd, 182–190 Wairau Road,
Auckland 10, New Zealand

Penguin Books Ltd, Registered Offices:
Harmondsworth, Middlesex, England

First published in the United States of America by
Louisiana State University Press 1983
Published in Penguin Books 1992

1 3 5 7 9 10 8 6 4 2

PUBLISHER'S NOTE
This is a work of fiction. Names, characters, places, and incidents either are the product of the author's imagination or are used fictitiously, and any resemblance to actual persons, living or dead, events, or locales is entirely coincidental.

THE LIBRARY OF CONGRESS HAS CATALOGUED THE HARDCOVER AS FOLLOWS:
Nooteboom, Cees, 1933–
Rituals: a novel.
Translation of: Rituelen.
I. Title.
PT5881.24.055R613 1983
839.3′1364 82–17278
ISBN 0-8071-1081-7 (hc.)
ISBN 0 14 01.5790 5 (pbk.)

Printed in the United States of America
Set in Linotron Galliard
Designed by Joanna Hill

PUBLISHER'S NOTE

The Pegasus Prize for Literature has been established by Mobil Corporation to introduce American readers to distinguished works from countries whose literature is rarely translated into English. *Rituals*, by Cees Nooteboom, was awarded the Pegasus Prize in the Netherlands in March, 1982, after a committee of distinguished scholars and editors selected it from among the best Dutch novels written in the past decade. The novel, written in 1980, has already won the Netherlands' prestigious F. Bordewijk Prize. In addition to four other novels, Mr. Nooteboom has also written several books of poetry and travel and one play.

The chairman of the Pegasus Prize selection committee was Joost de Wit, director of the Foundation for the Promotion of the Translation of Dutch Literary Works. Other members of the jury were Gerrit Borgers, head of the Dutch department, University of Amsterdam; Pierre Dubois, former editor, the *Vaderland*; Anton Korteweg, head curator of the Dutch Literary Museum; and Martin Mooy, organizer of Poetry International and head of the literary section of the Rotterdam Art Foundation.

In their summation of the jury report, the members cited *Rituals* for its "compelling narrative structure, the author's fascinating vision of the contemporary world and of a perceptive and sensitive individual's awareness of this world, and last but not least the excellence of the book's composition which, commensurate with its complexity, is at once lucid and penetrating."

This spare, incisive work is in three sections, each of which deals with the rituals that pervade the life of its hero, Inni Wintrop. In the first section, set in 1963, Wintrop is seen as an uncommitted, formerly Catholic, financially independent Dutch dilettante, emotionally detached from life and from his wife, Zita. In the second section, set in 1953, the young Inni grapples with questions of religion and identity; here, the symbolism of the trinity is played out against the tea ceremony, the dominant ritual of the final section, set in 1973. Throughout, Nooteboom is examining what he describes as the "moral geometry [that] defines our sense of proportion to the universe."

Rituals was originally published by the Amsterdam firm of De Arbeiderspers. It has been translated into English by Adrienne Dixon, who was born in Holland and now lives in England. Ms. Dixon's translations of Dutch and Flemish fiction won her the Martinus Nijhoff Prize for Translations in 1974.

On behalf of the author, we wish to express our appreciation to Mobil Corporation, which established the Pegasus Prize and provided for translation into English.

CONTENTS

Personne n'est, au fond, plus tolérant que moi. Je vois des raisons pour soutenir toutes les opinions; ce n'est pas que les miennes ne soient fort tranchées, mais je conçois comment un homme qui a vécu dans des circonstances contraires aux miennes a aussi des idées contraires.

Stendhal
"Brouillon d'article"

RITUALS

I INTERMEZZO 1963

Und allen Plänen gegenüber begleitet mich die Frage: "Was soll der Unsinn?"; eine Frage, die Überhaupt ganz und gar von mir Besitz zu nehmen droht.

Theodor Fontane

On the day that Inni Wintrop committed suicide, Philips shares stood at 149.60. The Amsterdam Bank closing rate was 375, and Shipping Union had slipped to 141.50. Memory is like a dog that lies down where it pleases. And that was what he remembered, if he remembered anything: the market reports and that the moon shone on the canal and that he had hanged himself in the bathroom because he had predicted, in his own horoscope in *Het Parool*, that his wife would run off with another man and that he, a Leo, would then commit suicide. It was a perfect prediction. Zita ran off with an Italian, and Inni committed suicide. He had read a poem by Bloem, too, but he could not remember which one. The dog, arrogant beast, let him down on this point.

Six years previously, on the eve of his marriage, he had wept, on the steps of the Palace of Justice on the same Prinsengracht, exactly such genuine tears as Zita had shed when he deflowered her in a room full of frogs and reptiles in the Valeriusstraat. And for the same reason. Dark premonitions, and an unfathomable dread of changing something, anything, in his life, if only by a mere sign or ceremony.

He loved Zita very much. In secret, only to himself, he called her the princess of Namibia. She did have green eyes, after all, and gleaming red hair and that dull pinkish-white complexion that goes with it—all features of the highest Namibian nobility—and she had that air of silent, reserved wonder that is regarded, in all the provinces of Namibia, as the true hallmark of the aristocracy.

Perhaps Zita loved Inni even more. It was only because Inni did not love himself that everything had gone wrong. There were, of course, people who claimed that it was because they both had such ridiculous names, but both Inni (Inigo, after the famous English architect) and Zita (the mother of the Namibian princess was a supporter of the House of Habsburg) knew that the strange sounds making up their names lifted them above, and isolated them from, the rest of the world. They could spend hours in bed saying Inni Inni, Zita Zita, and on special occasions also velvety variants—Zinnies, Itas, Inizitas, Zinnininitas, Itizitas—couplings of names and bodies that at such moments they would have wished to continue forever. But as no greater enmity exists than that between time in its entirety and each random, separate particle of time, there was no chance of that.

Inni Wintrop, fairly bald now but at that time blessed with springy, gold-colored hair that was long for those days, distinguished himself from many of his contemporaries by having difficulty in spending the night alone, by possessing a bit of money, and by sometimes having visions. For the rest he dealt in painting on occasion, wrote a horoscope for *Het Parool*, knew a great many poems by heart, and closely followed the stock and commodity markets. Political convictions, of whatever color, he regarded as more or less mild forms of mental illness, and he had reserved the role of dilettante, in the Italian sense of the word, for himself.

All this, seen as so many contradictions by those around him, was experienced in Amsterdam with increasing pain as the sixties began to unfold. "Inni lives in two worlds," said his friends, of all kinds and conditions, who themselves lived each in only one world. But Inni, who was ready to hate himself at any moment of the day, on request if need be, made an exception at this point. If he had ever had any ambition, he would have been prepared to call himself a failure, but he had none. He regarded life as a rather odd club of which he had accidentally become a member and from which one could be expelled without reasons having to be supplied. He had already decided to leave the club if the meetings should become all too boring.

But how boring is boring? Often it seemed that the moment had arrived. Inni would lie on the floor for days, his head pressed into the tormenting ribs of the Chinese rush mat, so that Fontana-like patterns appeared in his fairly soft skin. Wallowing, Zita called it, but she realized that it was genuine sorrow rising from deep and invisible springs, and on such somber days she looked after Inni as best she could. Usually the wallowing ended with a vision. Inni would then rise from the torments of the mat, beckon to Zita, and describe the apparitions he had just seen and what these had said to him.

Years had passed since the night in which Inni had wept on the steps of the Palace of Justice. Zita and Inni had eaten, drunk, and traveled. Inni had lost money dealing in nickel, made a profit in watercolors of the Hague school, and written horoscopes and recipes for *Elegance*. Zita had almost had a child, but on that occasion Inni had been unable to keep his fear of change under control and had given orders to prevent its entrance into a world for which, after all, he himself did not care much either. In so doing, he had put his signature under the biggest change of all, that Zita would leave him. Inni noticed only the first foreshadowings: her skin became drier, her eyes did not always look at him, she uttered his name less often. But he associated these signs only with her fate, not his.

It is a peculiarity of time that in retrospect it appears so compact, an indivisible solid object, a dish with only one smell and one flavor. Inni, familiar with the idiom of modern poetry, was fond of describing himself in those days as "a hole," an absence, a nonexistent. Unlike the poets, he did not mean anything specific by this. It was more a social comment on the fact that he was able to mix with the most diverse kinds of people. A hole, a chameleon, a being that could be given content, complete with attitude and accent—it was all the same to him, and Amsterdam offered every opportunity for mimicry. "You don't live," his friend the writer had once said to him, "you allow yourself to be distracted," and Inni had regarded this as a compliment. He thought he played his part equally well in a working-class bar and at a shareholders' meeting. Only his hairstyle and clothes posed a problem on occasion, but in the days when all Amsterdam became chameleonlike, when modes of dress proclaimed the anticipated classless society and it no longer mattered who wore what and when, Inni enjoyed the happiest time of his life, insofar as in his life there could be question of that.

Not so Zita. Even the limitless reserves of Namibia will become exhausted. There are women who are so faithful that nothing but a once-only unfaithfulness can save them from certain catastrophe. Inni might perhaps have been able to recognize this, but somewhere in the indivisible lump of never-to-be-recaptured time, he had ceased to pay attention to Zita. What was worse, he slept with her more and more often, heedless of all the omens, so that Zita gradually withdrew her love from this ever stranger man who, while exciting, caressing, and licking her, while bringing her off, would fail to notice her for days on end. Inni and Zita thus became two perfect lust machines, attractive to the eye, ornaments to the city, dream apparitions at the parties of Haffy Keizer and Dick Holthaus. When she was alone, Zita would sometimes linger by a window display of baby clothes. She would shudder with hidden revenge, usually at moments—only the great platonic computer that registers everything could observe this—when somewhere in a squalid room in some European capital Inni was having himself rubbed up by a whore or a teenager in jeans, or was making a killing at some gaming table by calling out banco six times in succession. To the cautiously advancing Mediterranean man who was attracted by the rapacious look on the white face in its frame of red hair reflected in the window of the baby store, Zita paid no attention. Her time had not yet come.

It was Amsterdam before the Provos, before the "dwarfs," before the long, hot summers. But at many places in that magic semicircle, unrest was sharpening. It seemed an age ago since the Indies had slipped away into one of those last pages of the Dutch history book that later would have to be rewritten so drastically. Korea had been divided with a ruler, by what some called the ineluctable course of history, and there were already people who knew that the seed of Vietnam had been sown. Fishes were beginning to die of things that fishes had not died of in the past, and the faces in the ever lengthening traffic jams along the canals displayed at times that mixture of frustration and aggression that was to make the seventies so unique. But as yet hardly anyone seemed to know that Nature, the mother of all, would soon waste away and that the end of our polluted era was at hand, for good.

And yet, under all this outward ignorance brewed the soft ferment of unrest, despair, and malice. The world had smelled foul for a long time and Amsterdam was beginning to smolder, but everyone blamed it on his own bad temper, worries, escapeless marriage, or lack of money. The great relief, that the disease was primarily that of the world and only secondarily of individual people, had not yet been offered by anyone.

"Ever gloomier, ever more awake" was Inni's device in those days. It was never quite clear when it was night for him, but he always woke up in the middle and then he died—at least, that was what he called it. It is well known that if a dying person has a moment to spare, however brief, he sees his life pass before him in a flash. This happened nightly to Inni, except that being scarcely able to remember his life up to the day his aunt Thérèse had appeared, all he saw was a gray film with an occasional sequence in which he, small or a little bigger, figured in brief, abrupt scenes. These were mostly unconnected incidents or lengthy stills of objects that for some inexplicable reason had been left behind in the empty attic of his memory, such as an egg on a plate in Tilburg or the enormous purple penis of a chance neighbor in a urinal at the Schenkkade in The Hague.

How it was that he could remember poems by heart was a mystery to him, and he often reflected that perhaps he would have done better to learn his life by heart so that in these recurring nocturnal last moments he could at least have watched an orderly film instead of all those loose fragments without the cohesion you might have expected of a life just ended. Perhaps the daily death was so immensely sad because no one was really dying at all. There was only a number of barely connected snapshots at which nobody would ever look. This unchangingly and relentlessly identical, meaningless cycle never bothered him during the daytime, because this kind of death did not really belong to that life. He was careful, therefore, not to talk of it with Zita or with anyone else. Zita slept a prehistoric, Namibian sleep, and when the hour of nocturnal suffering arrived, he detached himself from her total embrace, went to a different room, and wept bitterly though briefly. When he later climbed back into bed, her arms opened as if they saw him, but much more seemed to open—a whole Elysian world full of warm, soft meadows in which the hay had just been gathered and where all the Innis of the world were put to sleep.

* * *

His own lack of memory must have spread to other people, too. Otherwise it was inexplicable, thought Inni, that no one, but no one, was able to tell him later what kind of summer it had been in 1963. Summers, all of them, invariably reminded him of the woods around Arnold Taads's house near Doorn on a hot day: everything slightly hazy, sultry, there would be a thunderstorm soon, the lakes were black and dead silent and willing to reflect anything and everything, the ducks lay comatose in the reeds, on the roof of a country house a peacock screamed his cry of despair, and perhaps the universe was about to perish at last. Already there was a slight odor of decay, because nature itself wallowed. Inni did not have to do anything. That was what summers were like, and therefore also the summer of 1963, until someone checked up for him in old newspaper ledgers and told him that in 1963 it had rained constantly. He did remember, but it had been engraved on his mind that in that year he had fallen in love with a barmaid from the Voetboogsteeg and that an Italian migrant worker, employed in the kitchen of the Victoria Hotel but a photographer in his spare time, had taken a photograph of Zita for *Taboo*, a magazine that would last a mere two issues, just long enough to put an end to Inni and Zita's happiness. For whatever it was—the long wear and tear, the painstaking mutual consummation as if it were a perpetual meal, all those long Amsterdam nights of body migrations and sudden visions destined for an empty film reel—all of this together constituted happiness, and it was about to disappear, and it would never come back. Never.

The Voetboogsteeg bar was long and dark, designed for customers of the Exchange and provincials, low characters too craven to go to the whores and too stingy to keep a mistress. Instead, they came to the divine twilight in this Scotch-checkered bar to peer into Lyda's vast white bosom, a pleasure that had to be paid for with an unending stream of crème-de-menthe sodas. That had been the reason he fell in love, that slow river of green liquid disappearing into her wide mouth. That and the silver-gray sprayed, ludicrously tall hairdo, and those large white breasts of which so much and yet too little was visible, and the fact that she was more than a head taller than Inni. "I am all green inside," she used to say periodically, and that, too, excited him.

Since the first, real Lyda, who was not called Lyda but Petra, there had been many Lydas in Inni's life, and because he was not a consistent philosopher, he had several explanations for this. Sometimes it really had something to do with love, but at other times it happened that he regarded himself as a vampire who could live only if he could suck "light" out of women, passersby, or as he put it, undefined feminine beings of the female sex. These brief mountings, these exchanges, these mutual ministrations of almost nameless services, gave him temporarily the feeling that he existed after all. Not that he always found this agreeable. But sometimes, when time seemed never-ending, when the days confused him by their unimaginable duration, when it seemed as if there would always be more hours and minutes than water and air, he would go out into the street like a dog, simply disguising himself as someone in search of sex; and in the evening he would hide himself deeper than ever in Zita's arms. But there were also other times, days in which the hunter allowed himself to be hunted, times when objects were not so emphatically present and when he did not immediately, on seeing a car, think *car*, when the days did not hang around him like empty, never-to-be-filled vessels. At such times he was ecstatic. He would walk about the city as if he could fly, and abandon himself to anyone laying claim to a brief possession of Inni Wintrop.

Zita had no part in all this. He had decided that insofar as the world existed, and therefore he, too, he would have to obey Zita's code, which was a simple one: whatever he did, she did not want to know about it, since otherwise she would be obliged to kill him, and that would be of no benefit to anyone.

Suddenly, in the year we are talking of, it became November. Inni sold a small plot of land still left from his inheritance from his guardian, dined with the estate agent in the Oyster Bar, took Zita to a friend in Amsterdam South, and then offered Lyda a crème de menthe. "I'm seeing you home tonight," he said, deciding that this was a proper Amsterdam approach. "Are you now," she said, cocking her head like a parrot that wants to hear that same funny noise again. She took another sip, and as he saw the green liquid slithering in, Inni felt a slow excitement rising up from his toes.

Lyda lived in West. After the menthe, there had been the endless staircase to her attic, which had excited him immensely, and finally the room itself with the cane chair, the Nescafé, the marigolds, the coconut mat, and the framed portrait of her father, a bald Lyda, looking down suspiciously from the realm of the dead into the room, to see whom she had brought home this time. The nakedness of someone he had never seen naked before, Inni found touching. The fact that you could, with a few moves of the hand, somewhere in a wooden bird's nest on some floor or other in a nameless neighborhood, reduce a fully dressed, upright-walking stranger to the most natural state, that the person who a few moments earlier had been sitting in an espresso bar leafing through *Elsevier* was now lying naked beside you in a bed that had never existed before, though it had been in existence for years—if there was anything that could ward off death, blindness, and cancer, this was it.

Lyda was large and white and soft and full, and after the predictable course of events during which she had called out for her mother, the two of them looked like a failed attempt at flying, something sweaty that had crashed. Both of them were covered in a silvery layer of lacquer from her hair, which, after they had unpinned the candy-floss web, hung down to her hips. They lay still for a time. In accordance with the rules, Inni was sad. As he let the embrace with the bigger Lyda seep away into his memory gap, he felt, as usual, bitter at what was bound to happen next. They would disentangle themselves, maybe wash, he would descend the long staircase like someone descending a staircase, she would fall asleep in her own nest, tomorrow she would drink crème de menthe again, with idiots, and they would die, each one separately, in different hospital beds, ill treated by young nurses who were not yet born.

He groped behind him on the floor where, before getting into bed, he had seen a packet of Caballeros. As he half-raised himself and Lyda began to grunt softly under him, he suddenly looked into Zita's eyes. Paper eyes, but still Zita's. It was the photograph from *Taboo*, spread over two pages. Now, thought Inni, I am in Pompeii. The lava is pouring over me, and I shall stay like this forever. A man, half on top of a woman who, in the unthinkable "later," no one will know was not his wife, his head raised and looking at something that had become invisible forever. What he felt was sorrow. A hundred times he had seen this photograph, but now it was as if behind this portrait pinned to the brown wallpaper with four thumb tacks, there was a universe consisting only of Zita, which he would never be able to inhabit again. But what was it? Cool, green eyes cut from impenetrable stone. Had they ever looked at him with love? Her mouth stood slightly open as if she were about to say something, or had just said something that would forever put an end to Zita and Inni—a Namibian curse, an annihilating, soft-sounding formula. It would wipe out the juxtaposition of their ridiculous names and would banish him forever from her life, not only from the time that was still to come—that would be just bearable—but also from times already past, so that what had existed would then no longer exist. For eight years he would simply not have been there! He looked more and more intently at the paper face that every second changed further into an unfamiliar, rebuffing mask. There was no doubt that it saw him and therefore excluded him, because it was at the same time looking at someone else with the love that was no longer intended for him but for the only other person she had been looking at while the photograph was taken—the photographer.

"Nice noodle has that girl," said Lyda. She sat up. He saw that her breasts were now silver, too. The stuff was everywhere, on his face, his chest, her face, everywhere!

He stood up, saw his silver figure walk past the mirror, and got dressed.

"I don't want to get used to you," said Lyda, and it sounded like a point of order at a meeting.

He waved to the silvery, now suddenly tearstained blotch of her face and went out into the street of silent, death-feigning houses with their sleeping people. He drove straight to the city park and by a pond tried to wash the silver, the outward sign of his removal from Zita's life, from his hands. But he did not succeed, and it only became worse. Five o'clock passed. Nature, in which animals do not know one another and no one loves anyone, awakened.

A photographer, he thought, and remembered that he had first met Zita at a photographic exhibition, standing in front of a portrait of herself. He had seen the photo before he had seen her, and he did not know who betrayed whom, the woman in the photograph, the woman who stood before it, or the other way around. Some photographs, like that famous one of Virginia Woolf at the age of twenty, in which she looks sideways, are so perfect that the living being they represent seems a fabrication, something made so that a photograph may be taken of it. Inni had realized that if he wished to become acquainted with the woman in the photograph, he would have to address the woman standing in front of it, and this he had done. The photo hung in a rather dark corner, but he had at once been sucked toward it. Power emanated from it. It seemed as if that face, which could never really belong to a live human, had existed for thousands of years, independent of all else and completely absorbed in itself—an equilibrium.

He remembered clearly that he had begun to feel slightly dizzy as he approached her. She had walked away from her portrait, which made it easier, and stood by a window, a very soft layer of light all around her, alone. She had the total equanimity of someone who had been made solely to be different from the others without ever being conscious of it, a different order of being that consisted of only one member—her. And so he had entered her world without ever becoming a member of it, and he had wrought damage in it while refreshing himself on the perfect equilibrium. And now he was about to be punished for it.

Slowly it grew lighter. He shivered with cold. A large heron flew over, lurched, and then landed in the reeds with clattering wing movements. For the rest all was silent, and it seemed to Inni as if he were standing still for the first time, as if since that first meeting with Zita he had never stopped walking and had come all the way here in one long haul, in one movement, in order to stand by this pond with silver smudges on his hands and, who knows, on his face, too. He decided not to remove them and to go home at once.

If everything he was thinking was true, he would have to be punished now, and the sooner the better. Nothing was sure any longer. This, then, was chaos, and chaos was what frightened him most in life—the chaos into which he would be flung back if she left him.

It did not turn out the way he had thought. Of course Zita was in love with the photographer and of course she had slept with him. He had been her first man since she had been with Inni, just as Inni had been the first man in her life. With the absolute certainty of someone who lives by laws, she now knew she would have to leave Inni, and because she loved him and knew of his dread of chaos, this grieved her. But there was nothing to be done about it. It would happen the way it happens in Namibia, without a sound, swiftly, and without a single crack in the crystal. She kissed him when he came in, said that she had something to wash off that funny silver with, helped him remove it, stood close against him, and took him into bed with her. Never had he loved her so much. He would have liked to push first his head and only then all the rest right inside her and stay there forever. But when it was all over and she was asleep like a newborn sister of Tutankhamen, so terrifyingly still as if she had not breathed for centuries, as if she had not only such a short while before been a frenzied, shouting maniac, he knew that he had discovered nothing about his fate.

She was absent, as he had been all these years. He got up and took a sleeping tablet from his stock. But when he awoke in the early afternoon, she was still the same as in the morning, as last year and the year before—a marsh of perfection into which anyone who ventured too far for the first time would drown.

The weeks passed. Zita saw her Italian, slept with him, let herself be photographed by him. And each time another photo was taken, another fleck of Inni dissolved into the air of Amsterdam. The new love was the crematorium of the old. So it happened that one day, as Inni was walking across the Koningsplein, a speck of ashes floated into his eye which would not come out until Zita licked it away with the tip of her tongue and said he did not look well.

That was one Friday afternoon, and what was to happen next had little to do with Italians and with love, but rather with a subterranean, unwritten Namibian law mysteriously handed down through the ages—a law according to which accounts must be settled once every eight years, but then for good on a Friday afternoon. On such afternoons there must be men in that country who are doomed to die a terrible death. But as with so many ancient customs, the sharper edges had worn away in the diaspora. Inni would be banished, but that it would happen on this particular day he did not know. Zita had made her calculations and she no longer belonged to Inni. That day she would leave for Italy with her Italian, who like her had no money. What would happen there she did not know, and she somehow had a feeling that it did not concern her. It would happen, that was what mattered.

After she had licked the speck of ashes from Inni's eye, he sat down at his desk. He had an hour and a half to hand in his horoscope at *Het Parool* for the Saturday supplement. He leafed through *Marie Claire*, *Harper's Bazaar*, *Nova*, and his books of stars. He copied something here, invented something there, and busied himself with the destinies of other people because they were going to read it. When he arrived at his own constellation, Leo, he had just read in *Harper's* that things would go well with him and in *Elle* that the outlook was somber. He put down his pen and said to Zita, who had lain down on the settee by the window in order to look out over the Prinsengracht for the last time, "Why are you never allowed to write, Dear Cancer, you will get cancer, or Leo, something dreadful will happen to you today, your wife will leave you and you will commit suicide?" Zita knew he was now thinking of his aunt and of Arnold Taads, and the green of her eyes darkened, but he did not notice and chuckled. She turned her head toward him and looked at him. A total stranger was sitting at a desk, grinning. She laughed. Inni stood up and went toward her. He stroked her hair and wanted to lie down beside her.

"No," she said, but this in itself meant nothing. It could be part of a game in which she had to, or wanted to, taunt him or in which he had to tell her a story.

"This time you have to pay," she said. That was not new either. He felt a great desire rising in him.

"How much?" he asked.

"Five thousand guilders."

He laughed. Five thousand guilders. He unbuttoned her blouse.

The most he had ever paid her was a hundred guilders. They always had to laugh at that. Usually they would lie on top of the bank note so that they could hear it rustling. She always showed him later what she had bought with it, or she invited him out to dinner somewhere, and once she had, with her serenest look, walked into the house of a whore in the red-light district and had handed over the money without a word.

"Five thousand guilders," repeated Zita. "Your checks are in the red cupboard." This was a new game. It excited him madly, but she did not smile. Or was that what was new?

"All right," he said.

The squaring of accounts, the settlement of a debt, the final payment for absence, the ultimate obliteration of a love, the swallowing up of all the time between that first glimpse at the photographic exhibition and the present moment, still involving the same two bodies, now began to take shape.

Many years later, when he would meet her again in a shabby hotel room in Palermo, he would ask her why, and she would not answer him because she knew he knew. Now, while that hotel room already existed but not yet the years that they would spend away from each other, he fetched the checks from the red cupboard and signed them. She accepted them from him, still without a smile, got up and went to a corner of the room, where she took her wallet out of her handbag. She carefully slid the checks into it, put the bag down, and still without smiling and with a frightening nonpresence that was a punishment but that may still have been part of a new game, she slowly undressed. She stood naked, looking at him, went to the bed, lay down, closed her eyes, and said, "Go on then." Already, and they knew it although they could not see it, there flowed in that room in Palermo, very softly, very gently, that which was the reason for which she would leave him and had left him—his weakness.

* * *

He undressed with that same hole-and-corner feeling he also had with real whores. She put her right hand to her mouth and made herself wet. Come, she said, but what did she want, he thought. That he would really treat her like a whore, or get so angry (pretend to get angry) that he would rape her (pretend to rape her)?

"I can't, like this," he said.

"You always can," she said. She put her hands on his neck and pushed his head beside her on the pillow so that they would not have to see each other. And so, a blind man mating with a blind woman, he came inside her for the last time in a great annihilating silence that still continued when she pulled away from underneath him and walked out of the room with her hand between her legs.

Inni stayed behind. He was aware of a great coldness, of fear and humiliation. Like someone, he thought, returning from a journey and finding his house full of broken glass, shit, and rubbish. While he lay wondering what to do, Zita phoned the bank from the other room and told them to stay open a few minutes longer because she had to collect a large sum in lire. Meanwhile, Inni's seed ran into the hand between her legs and fell through her fingers onto the floor. He heard her dressing and walking about the room, determined the direction of her steps, first barefooted, then in shoes, heard her briefly pausing by the threshold, hesitating, returning toward him, for a moment only and then no longer, and heard her say, already at the door, "Remember your horoscope, four o'clock is the deadline." And then he heard only the door and the November wind briefly chasing through it.

He sat down at his desk and finished the horoscope.

Through Utrechtsestraat, Keizersgracht, Spiegelstraat, Herengracht, Koningsplein, he reached *Het Parool*'s office on the Nieuwezijds, where he handed in his piece. And while Zita was on her way from the bank in the Vijzelstraat to the coffee house outside

Central Station, where she had arranged to meet her Italian, Inni, immeasurably more slowly, walked homeward in the opposite direction. He stopped at Scheltema's, the Koningshut, Hoppe's, Pieper's, at Hansel and Gretel's, and at the Centrum Café. Never before had he been so drunk. It was night when he got home. He called out her name in the empty house and went on calling until the neighbors phoned to tell him to shut up. Only then did he find the note saying she was never going to come back, and as he held it in his hand and stared at it, he heard his own voice. "Leo, something dreadful will happen to you today, your wife will leave you and you will commit suicide." He knew what to do. He swayed about the room, knocking into chairs and tables, and went to the bathroom to hang himself, with some difficulty, from the highest point, where the central heating conduit and the water pipe were joined by a double ring before they disappeared into the ceiling.

The sky of death was a sky of gray clouds. They chased across the treetops along the canal. He woke up in a bed full of vomit, and with trembling fingers removed the tie from his neck. All over his body there were grazes, and there was blood on the sheet. As if someone had wound up a mechanism, he went to the bathroom, washed, shaved, took two Alka-Seltzers, refused to think of Zita, and left the house. On the corner of the Utrechtsestraat he bought a copy of the *Handelsblad*. He walked to Oosterling's, where he asked for two black coffees, and as usual, he turned to the financial pages first. The letters were bigger than usual, and slowly, as if he had suddenly grown much older, he read what it said. "At the urgent request of the Board of the Association of Stockbrokers, business closed at 20.45 following the death of the American president. After the appalling news that President Kennedy had been seriously, probably fatally injured, prices fell rapidly. The Dow-Jones average, which had initially risen by 3.31, fell to 711.49. This means a loss of 21.16 compared with Thursday's closing rate and is the sharpest drop since the panic wave on 28 May 1962."

He folded the paper and glanced for a moment at the photograph on the front page. The youthful president lay asleep on the rear seat of his huge car. The woman with the Oresteia mask at his side was standing up straight, staring at the large wine stains on her forever unforgettable costume. Of three things Inni was certain: Zita would never come back, he was not dead, and tomorrow the stock market would be spinning like a top. On the gold that he would buy the following Monday through his broker in Switzerland, he would, by 1983 when this fateful picture appeared for the ten thousandth time in all the weeklies of the world, have made more than a thousand percent profit. The photograph was clear indeed: confused times were at hand.

II ARNOLD TAADS 1953

Simili modo postquam coenatum est, accipiens et hunc praeclarum Calicem in sanctas ac venerabiles manus suas; item tibi gratias agens, benedixit, deditque discipulis suis, dicens: Accipite, et bibite omnes. Hic est enim Calix sanguinis mei, novi et aeterni testamenti: mysterium fidei: qui pro vobis et pro multis effundetur in remissionem peccatorum. Haec quotiescumque feceritis, in mei memoriam facietis.

Likewise after supper He took this illustrious Cup into his holy and venerable hands, and when he had given thanks again he blessed it and gave it to his disciples saying: "Take this and drink ye all of this. For this is the cup of my Blood, of the new and everlasting testament, the mystery of faith, which is shed for you and for many for the remission of sins. Do this often as ye shall drink it, in remembrance of Me."

From the canon of the Holy Mass

Until he met Philip Taads, Inni Wintrop had always thought that Arnold Taads was the loneliest man in the Netherlands. So it could be even worse. Here was someone who had had a father, true, but who had derived no benefit from the fact. Arnold Taads had never mentioned a son, thereby, thought Inni, condemning that son to a curious form of nonexistence which eventually led to that definitive form of nonexistence which is death.

Since father and son had, in complete isolation from each other and without consultation, opted for absolute absence, their only manifestation, as far as Inni was concerned, was possibly a presence in his thoughts. They made use of this fairly often. At the most unexpected hours and places they would loom up in his dreams or in those half-waking thoughts that are sometimes called reveries, and what they had never done during their lifetimes they did now: they appeared together, an unreal duo coming to his hotel room at night to frighten him with their all-destroying sadness.

His first encounter with Arnold Taads he would remember as long as he lived, if only because the memory was inextricably linked with his aunt Thérèse, who herself had also committed suicide, albeit not in so planned a manner as the other two.

Only a few people per thousand commit suicide, a random little group such as you may see in the Lairessestraat in Amsterdam, waiting for the number 16 tram just before the rush hour. The peak of this statistic appeared to be in his vicinity, and statistics were infallible. From the number of self-murderers he had known—you had to put it that way, for the fact that someone died rounded off your knowledge of that person, if only because he or she could no longer present you with surprises—he was able to conclude that his circle of acquaintance must consist of a thousand people. If he were to invite all these voluntary dead to tea, two boxes of cream cakes from Berkhof's would scarcely suffice.

He divided the departed into two kinds, according to their method: slide and stairs. The first went, after some initial difficulty, automatically, while for the other method some exertion was needed.

Aunt Thérèse had gone by slide, that was certain. Drink and an infallible mixture of hysteria and lethargy had shown her the exit from the ballroom as if of its own accord, while the two Taadses had struggled tenaciously through whole labyrinths, interminably climbing stairs, finally to end up at the same point.

Inni Wintrop was one of those people who drag the time they have spent on earth behind them like an amorphous mass. This was not a thought he entertained daily, but one that recurred regularly and that already used to occupy him when he had had a considerably shorter past to carry about.

He was unable to estimate the time, measure it, divide it up. Perhaps it would be better to leave out the article here and say *time*, so as to give it all the tough syrupyness to which it is entitled. Nor was it only the past that clung to Inni's spoon in this manner; the future, too, was stubborn. A similarly formless space awaited him there, to be traversed by him without any clear indication as to which route he should take to get out of it. One thing was certain: the time he had lived was finished, but now that he was forty-five and had, by his own account, "crossed the frontier into the terrible without ever having been asked to show his passport," this amorphous thing containing both his memory and his lack of memory continued to accompany him as mysteriously and, even in reverse direction, as immeasurably as the universe about which there was so much discussion these days.

Somewhere in the gray milky mist of the early fifties, in which the vigorous white bloom of the Korean War was still visible, there must have occurred that moment, less easily perceived, alas, when his aunt Thérèse (*treize*, Thérèse, *ne perd jamais*), from whom a few years later he would inherit the foundation of his relative prosperity, had made her appearance in his lodgings at the Trompenbergerweg in Hilversum.

What made exercising his memory difficult was not only the fact that his apparatus was so limited ("I have no memory . . . You have clearly repressed everything . . . Can't you ever remember anything, for god's sake!") but also that, as he grew older, the available supports and footholds needed for a trip to the underworld of the past were beginning to disappear. That aunt Thérèse had exchanged her tangible flesh for the blurred shadow which from time to time roamed through a dimly lit corridor of his brain was bad enough, as was the fact that the driver of the white Lincoln convertible had been killed in a crash together with the uncle who belonged to aunt Thérèse. But worse than this was that the lodging house in which Inni had spent the first few years of his adult life had sunk without trace, together with his memories, into the hole from which would rise a clutch of eight service flats and which had sucked even the hydrangeas, chestnuts, larches, rhododendrons, and jasmines down into the depths from which nothing ever returns.

Nothing?

Those large, decaying houses, built once upon a time by former colonials, were themselves repositories of memories from an equally indisputably decayed era. They bore such names as *Terang-Tenang* or *Madura*, and the skinny, nervous, romantic Inni of those days could, especially in the soft fragrance of a summer evening, imagine himself to be living on a plantation somewhere near Bandung, an impression strengthened further by the presence of colonial old-timers who had their lodgings in that same, ridiculously large house. The smells of tropical food wafted through the villa, and there was a shuffling of slow slippers on the rush mats in the corridor, tongue clicking, and high, soft, strangely drawling voices saying things he did not understand but which he associated with books he had read by Couperus, Daum, and Dermout.

He hated his photographs from those days, not so much the ones in which he appeared together with other people—everyone looked equally ridiculous in those—no, the ones in which the attention could not be diverted from the person he had obviously been. He was on his own, posing, grim, imitating some statue and at the same time seeking the support of a tree, a gate, or any object that would presently occupy at least part of the picture so that he would not have to fill it all by himself. For what would such a photograph show? Someone so thin that he had been rejected for military service and, what was worse, who dared not therefore undress on a beach, someone who had been expelled from four different high schools and had quarreled with his guardian so that the allowance his grandmother had so generously agreed to pay him had been stopped, someone who lost himself in the most desperate infatuations and spent his days in an office to be able to pay for his lodgings. A person of minimal independence.

This was how it must have been, more or less: he was sitting in his room when his landlord's Indonesian voice called him from the corridor.

"Misterr Wintrrop, therr is a lady here to see you."

A moment later she was standing in his room, which was difficult enough, because it was really too cramped for two people and she was almost two all by herself.

"I am your aunt Thérèse," she said.

"You are a real Wintrop," she said.

She edged past him, briefly enveloping him in a soft, musklike scent, and looked out of the window. She did not like what she saw. Her next utterances did not so much come in a logical sequence but as a staccato run, all in the same tone. "He reads books. How small it is in here. I have heard about you. You can't turn your backside in here. My God, this place makes me feel gloomy. Has anybody ever told you about me? We'll go for a drive. I'll introduce you to someone who writes books." She said *writes* with such emphasis that it was clear she regarded this as an activity far superior to reading.

It was Saturday afternoon, and springtime. Later he reflected that she never asked him if he wanted to come. They simply went, or rather, she breezed down the stairs, flew through the garden as if it were a hostile element, fled into the car, and said, "We're going to see Mr. Taads, Jaap."

The car tore away. She had nothing to do all day—this too had dawned on him only later—but did it with the greatest possible speed. In his innocence he still thought that her excitement was perhaps caused by certain mysterious chemical processes somewhere in that white, slightly bloated body, as if a saucepan full of her blood was constantly on the boil on an internal stove. Blotches of different colors appeared and disappeared on the skin of her face and neck, and if she had not regularly heaved one of her big sighs, she would surely have exploded.

What was a Wintrop? he wondered, for she kept talking about that.

"All Wintrops are mad, wicked, vain, they lack discipline, they live in confusion, they are constantly getting divorced. They treat their wives like cattle and yet these women remain in love with them, they are on the wrong side in the war or they make money out of it, they are crafty in business but they gamble their money away or throw it in the air, and they'll sell one another for a few pence. Did you ever know your father?"

She did not wait for his answer.

"You were christened, did you know that? My brother was a resistance hero, an exception in this highly principled family. The same cannot be said of your father. He had no idea how to handle money. Women, that was all he knew anything about. Do you still go to church?"

To this at least he was able to answer.

"No."

"Jaap, stop here a moment."

The white Lincoln shot up on the curb, narrowly missing a cyclist. She looked straight at him. Blue eyes, like his. Watery but with a steel bottom. With her finger she pointed roughly to where his heart must be.

"The Wintrops are a Catholic family. A Catholic Brabant family. The only one of your father's brothers who has remained in the church is the one who has all the money. Your father, your uncle Jos, your uncle Noud, your uncle Pierre, your aunt Claire, they're all either dead or they're on their uppers. You have nothing apart from what you may get from your grandmother one day. They all left the church, chasing after some skirt. You think about that."

Within a minute they were doing over seventy again.

The trip, it turned out, took them to the village of Doorn. But not only to Doorn. If there existed a map of the underworld, of the world of shadows, then Doorn lay at its entrance. For this drive to Doorn was a drive to his family's past, to bygone names and people, to the Tilburg of the turn of the century, to woolen textiles, to agencies, to manufacturers. Her accent broadened. The Tilburg dialect must be the ugliest in the Netherlands. He listened to her tales and stored them in his mind. Later he would think about them. Later.

"Your mother was never received by us. You know why?"

"She told me." So that was what the accent reminded him of: his mother when she was agitated. So in Tilburg the common people and the bourgeoisie spoke alike.

"Do you still see her?"

"Never. She doesn't live in Europe."

Three weeks after marrying the daughter of a French business connection, his father had run off with his mother. Which the family had regarded as worse, the mortal sin or the misalliance, could not be ascertained. They had forgotten his father afterwards, but with the kind of forgetfulness whereby you forget what you have forgotten. The glove you left on a train, of which you never think again. He knew the whole story, but it had never been of any significance. A future girlfriend would say to him one day, "I was never born, I was founded," and he had recognized this. His father had been in the underworld since 1944, and his death had cut Inni out of the family twice over. He knew hardly any of his relations. He did not belong anywhere, and this suited him splendidly. He was alone. He did not know what it was, to have relations.

"Your grandfather Wintrop and my father were half-brothers. My father is your guardian."

"Was."

"He was afraid you would cost him money. We don't like that. He could get out of it quite easily, being a governor of the Child Welfare Board."

Money or God, who was to say. Inni had seen him once. A gray man in an armchair beneath his own portrait as a governor, a diamond ring on each of his little fingers—but that was all right when you were old and ugly—and a hand bell within reach ("Treezy, give my nephew a glass of port"). The story of his grandmother's money ("I shall manage it for you to the best of my ability") had not become clear to Inni, nor had it been a happy interview in other respects. Inni, pointing with thin, long hands and speaking in his sharp, northern boy's voice, had explained why God did not exist.

"We only became Catholics later. Those are the best ones. Originally we were a Protestant military family. The first Wintrop to come to Tilburg was a lieutenant colonel in the lancers. They came from the Westland."

Fables, thought Inni, lies and fables. Invented characters from an invented past. Because your own life is too dreary.

"He arrived here with the bodyguard of Willem the Second, who built the town hall and palace where he never lived, and he married a Catholic girl."

The word *girl* stirred him. So there had been, in other centuries, girls who had been relations of his. Invisible girls who, with girls' mouths that he had never seen, had pronounced their surname, his.

"Ever since that time the Wintrops have been in textiles. Woolens. Tweeds. Factories. Agencies."

More shadows still. People who had the right to course in his blood, to dwell in his shoulders, his hands, his eyes, his facial features, because they had procreated him.

The car sliced the landscape in two, tossing it casually backwards. It made him feel as if the life he had been leading these last few years was being flung away at the same time. His aunt remained silent for a while. He saw the blood throbbing in the blue veins of her wrists and thought *my blood*, but on his own wrists nothing was to be seen.

"Arnold Taads was once my lover," said his aunt. She started applying makeup to her face. It was not an attractive sight. She spread a second skin of orange-colored pancake on top of the first, slack white skin, but she did not do it very accurately, so that narrow strips of white remained visible between the streaks of orange.

"I met him the other day for the first time since the war."

He could not conjure up any visual image of a lover of this woman, and when he saw Arnold Taads, he understood why. Someone who looked like that he never could have visualized, because he had never seen anyone like that.

He was a short man, standing in the doorway of the low, white house that lay half-hidden in the woods, and was looking at his watch. He had a glass eye—the right one—wore tall bushranger's boots and an old Red Indian jacket with long chamois fringes. This was in those long-forgotten days when people still wore suits and ties. The man's face was brown, but close beneath his conspicuous health seethed something else, a grayer, sadder element. One eye and no eye, a healthy and an unhealthy skin, a booming voice out of a grim, domineering face, a voice which had been meant for a larger body than that which housed it.

"You are ten minutes early, Thérèse."

At that moment an enormous dog appeared behind him and shot out into the garden.

"Athos! Come here!"

This voice was loud enough to command a battalion. The dog stood still, trembling in his skin of dark brown curly hair. Then he lowered his head and slowly went back into the house, past his master. The man himself turned and went inside. The white door fell shut behind him, softly and decisively.

"His dog, his dog," complained his aunt. "He lives for his dog."

She looked at her watch. From the house came piano music, but

Inni could see nothing through the windows. It did not sound very good. Too sharp, too stiff, without luster. Music which was intended to flow, but which instead jolted and halted, music which this person should not have been allowed to play. But who would? Someone with two glass eyes, or someone with an unhealthy, gray skin, or a small man with a soft, brown skin. Someone different.

"We'll go for a stroll," said his aunt, but he soon found that she was not up to it. On the other side of the avenue lay a wood. A scent of honeysuckle and young pine trees. His aunt Thérèse kept twisting her ankles in the soft sand of the path. She bumped into trees, stumbled over a fallen branch, became entangled in a bramble bush. For the first time that afternoon he felt fear. What did it all mean? He had not asked for this. Dragged from the quiet universe of his room, hustled into a family which, admittedly, was his but for which he had never cared in the least, having a door shut in his face by a man who should really have been two people. And a chauffeur. Leaning against the preposterously big car and probably laughing, he stood watching his employer stumbling a hundred meters and then gave a soft clarion call on the horn to announce that the ten minutes were up.

Da capo. The man was standing in the doorway again. Everyone had grown ten minutes older. This has already happened, thought Inni. The same formation, the eternal Second Coming. His aunt was in front of him, a little to one side, so that the man could see him. But the man did not look. Nor did he glance at his watch this time, for everyone knew what the time was anyway. The straight gray beam of the one eye roved like a searchlight over the person of Thérèse Donders. Of the three men present, only the chauffeur knew that her white two-piece suit, covered with pine needles and hairy thorny twigs, was handmade by Coco Chanel.

"Hello, Thérèse, what a sight you look."

Only then did the man look at Inni. Perhaps it was because of that single eye that the target had a feeling of being photographed by a camera whose aim could not miss, which sucked him up, swallowed him, developed him, and then put him away for good in an archive that would cease to exist only when the camera died.

"This is a nephew of mine."

"I see. My name is Arnold Taads." The hand closed around his like a vice.

"What is his name?"

"Inni."

"Inni . . . " the man let the ridiculous name hover in the air for a moment, then flicked it away. Inni told him the origin of his name.

"In your family everyone is mad," said Arnold Taads. "Come in."

The orderliness that reigned in the room was frightening. The only form of accident was the dog, because he moved. It was, thought Inni, a room like a mathematical problem. Everything was in equilibrium, each thing fitted in with the other. A bunch of flowers, a child, a disobedient dog, or a visitor arriving ten minutes early would wreak inconceivable havoc here. All the furniture was gleaming white, of a vindictive, Calvinist modernity. The irresponsible sunlight drew geometric shadows on the linoleum. For the second time that afternoon he felt fear. What kind? As if, just for a moment, you are someone else, someone who cannot get used to being inside your body, so that it hurts.

"Sit down. Thérèse, you'll want a manzanilla. And what will your nephew drink?"

And then, directly to Inni, "Will you have a whiskey?"

"I've never tried it," said Inni.

"Good. Then I will pour you a whiskey. You will taste it carefully and then you will tell me what you think of it."

Memory. The mysterious ways thereof. For what happened in the following five minutes? First, there was literally the very first, material whiskey—the glass of whiskey that he would never drink again. Second, there was the man he would so often think of, later in his life, when he saw, drank, and tasted whiskey. Of that man, and therefore of his aunt, and therefore of himself. In this way the whiskey had become his madeleine, the handle on the trapdoor that has to be lifted for the great descent into the shadow world. And they will sit there again: the man erect, his single dreadful eye aimed straight at him, the hand which has poured the soda still on its return journey to a resting place closer to its owner. His aunt slouches, head leaning backward, eyes vacant, roving, legs stretching, opening, closing, on the too straight, too hard chair. A dolorosa. Himself he cannot see.

"Well, how does it taste?" A definition was demanded from him, a protocol his senses were required to formulate before they could be distracted by any other sensation.

"Of smoke, and of hazelnut."

Thousands of whiskeys he has drunk since. Malt, bourbon, rye, the best and the worst, straight, with water, with soda, with ginger ale. And sometimes, suddenly, that sensation would come to him again. Smoke—yes, and hazelnut.

At each important moment in your life, he thought later, you ought to have an Arnold Taads, someone who asks you to describe exactly what you feel, smell, taste, and think when you experience your first fear, your first humiliation, your first woman. But the question must be asked always at the moment itself so that the protocol remains valid and the thought, the experience, can never be discolored by later women, fears, humiliations. Precisely that definition of the first time—smoke and hazelnut—would set the tone for all future experiences, for they would be determined by the extent to which they either deviated from that first time, which had now become the yardstick for the future, or fell short of it, being no longer smoke or hazelnut. To see Amsterdam for the first time again, to enter the loved one with whom you have lived for years for the first time again, to hold a woman's breast in your hand for the first time again and to stroke it, and to keep the thoughts relating to this intact through the years, so that all those later times, all those other forms, cannot in due course betray, deny, cover up, that first sensation.

Arnold Taads had at least set a standard on one sensuous experience for him. All the others would vanish irrevocably in later layers of his memory, interblended and corrupted in the way that his hand, which had caressed that first breast and closed those first dead eyes, had betrayed his memory, himself, and that first breast by having become older and misshapen. It was a hand showing the first brown freckles of old age, with thick veins, a corrupted, tainted, experienced forty-five-year-old hand, an early harbinger of death in which that former, slenderer, whiter hand had dissolved unrecognizably, unfindably, while he still called it "my hand," and would continue to do so until a later, living hand would lay it, dead, on his breast, crossed over the other that resembled it.

"What do you do?" asked Arnold Taads.

"I work in an office."

"Why?" This belonged to the class of superfluous questions.

"To earn money."

"Why aren't you a student?"

"I haven't got a high school diploma. I was expelled from school." He had been expelled from four schools, but it did not seem the right moment to divulge this. The eye, which had been fixed on him uninterruptedly, now moved without the head in which it was lodged turning with it, like a searchlight to his aunt, so that Inni was free to let his gaze wander about the room. On the mantelpiece lay twenty packets of cigarettes all of the same brand, Black Beauty. Beside them stood a number of silver and gold medals on a stand, each representing a skier.

"What are those medals?" asked Inni.

"We're talking about you now. Don't forget, I used to be a notary. I always finish things properly. What do you want to be in life?"

"I don't know."

He realized that this was not a good answer, but it was the only possible one, even to someone who liked to finish things properly. He had not the faintest idea. As a matter of fact, he was sure that not only did he never want to be anything but that he never would be anything either. The world was already chock-full of people who were something, and most of them were clearly not happy with what they were.

"Do you want to stay in that office then?"

"No."

Office! An upstairs room in a residential area, with a madman on the ground floor who thought he was the director of something and who needed him to be his staff. The man bought and sold something, and Inni wrote the letters to and from. Letters of air, business without substance. Usually he spent the day reading, looking out over the back garden, or thinking of distant journeys—without much yearning, for he knew he would make them anyway some time. It was an existence which would stop all by itself one day, and perhaps this was that day.

"Don't your parents give you any money?"

"My mother hasn't got any and my . . . my stepfather doesn't give me any."

Smoke and hazelnut. What do you want to be? On that afternoon his life had begun, and he had never become anything. He had done things, certainly. Traveled, written horoscopes, sold paintings. Later, with that glass of whiskey in his hand still recurring in the realm of his memory, he thought that that was precisely it: his life had consisted of incidents, but these were not coordinated into any kind of idea about his life. There was no central thought, such as a career, an ambition. He simply existed, a son without a father and a father without a son, and things just happened. In fact, his life consisted in manufacturing memories, and it was therefore all the more regrettable that he had such a bad memory, because this made his already fairly long voyage even longer; all those empty gaps gave it an almost unbearable slowness sometimes. So he told his friend the writer that his life was a meditation. Was it because of the glass of whiskey or because on that afternoon he had become a Wintrop financially that he regarded his life as having started on that day, and all that had gone before as a preamble, as half-dark prehistory into which only excavations could provide any insight at all, assuming anyone wanted to bother?

"Thérèse, why don't you give the boy some money? Your family took everything away from his father."

The red blotches multiplied. It had begun as a whim, an attack of family-mania inspired by boredom, this visit to the unknown nephew who looked as if he might be something special, who had contradicted her father. He now sat here with a face like many of the others wandering about the pages of her photo album, though probably with a personality different from most. He was not free from arrogance or from melancholy; he was articulate but clearly without ambition; and he was doubtlessly lazy, intelligent, mocking, and constantly observing. And now, her whim must be translated into hard matter, and to be precise, into the kind of matter from which the Wintrops were least happy to part—money.

"I would have to see if I can raise anything," she said. "You know what it's like with these things."

But it had been a commanding voice that had laid down the law, the same voice that would say, as soon as she had gone, "She is a stupid woman, and she pesters me, which is what I can't stand."

She readjusted something invisible in her lap and overturned an imaginary vase, actions that froze when Arnold Taads's voice continued: "I shall think of a fair arrangement. One doesn't let people of one's own kind waste their time in offices."

"Will you come to Goirle with him then, next weekend?"

"You know I hate going there and that I find your husband's company hard to bear, but yes, I will come. I shall bring Athos with me, but on no account will I go to church. If you send the car, we shall be ready to leave at eleven o'clock on Saturday."

The eye sought Inni.

"And you hand in your notice, because that job of yours is pointless, that is obvious. You should spend a year reading or traveling. You are not suited to be a subordinate."

Sub-or-di-nate. A word of four syllables was indeed given, by this voice, four individually wrapped, separate doses of emphasis. Not a single word, thought Inni, of what the man had said during the afternoon had yet vanished from the room. Like objects they were stacked away somewhere among the furniture. There was no escape any more.

"Well, Thérèse, it is nearly five o'clock. My reading hour. Your nephew can stay for dinner here if he wants to. I'll see you on Saturday. Tell your chauffeur to be on time."

She rushed out of the room. He saw her flying down the garden path and heard the car moving off fast. He wiped away the wetness her fleeting kiss had left on his cheek. Arnold Taads returned to the room. Somewhere in the house a clock struck five. He picked up a book and said: "I read until a quarter to six. Amuse yourself."

An iron silence settled on the bungalow. Inni knew exactly what kind of silence it was, for he had heard it before, in a Trappist monastery. The knock on the door, the shuffling, the smothered rustle of heavy cloth in the corridors, the footsteps, soft as if in snow. Then the entrance into the chapel, the dry wooden tap starting a half-hour of communal meditation. Spellbound, he had looked down from the visitors' gallery onto the white, immobile figures in the cold, tall choir stalls below. Old men, young men, chewing on some thought or other, forever inaccessible to him. On one occasion he had seen one of the men fall asleep, slowly toppling forward like a piece of wood. Another dry tap had sounded, stone on wood. The man, startled from his stupor, had scrambled to his feet and come forward on the black-and-white checkered stone floor between the rows of choir stalls, bowed, but *bowed*, broke in two before the abbot, who wordlessly, with a sign, dealt him his punishment—prostration. The long, white figure fell to the ground like a dead swan, his hands as far from his feet as possible, a flattened, humiliated being, stretched out full length. And not one of all those men had looked up. Only the tap of stone on wood, the abbot's ring, a few footsteps, the rustle of clothes had broken the silence.

Now he was again in a monastery, the monastery of one man, his own monk and his own abbot.

Inni needed to go to the bathroom but dared not move. Or would the man, on the contrary, despise him if he sat here all the time like a dummy, without doing anything? Slowly and very quietly he got up, walked past the reading man, who did not look up—on the cover he saw existentialism . . . humanism—towards the piano—Schubert . . . impromptu—and from there out into the corridor. In the bathroom he found a copy of the *Haagse Post*, which he took back to the living room. He turned the loose pages as if they must not displace any air and read the anecdotes he would be reading all his life. After the Iranian rebellion Egypt was at the top of the list of sensitive trouble spots for the West. *Pravda*, in a long fierce article, attacked the Bermuda Conference, which President Eisenhower had convened to discuss whether one ought to talk with the Kremlin, as Sir Winston favored, or stand firm, as President Eisenhower recommended. The French president Vincent Auriol had asked Paul Reynaud to form a new government. History.

How many names would have to settle inside him, flow through him, until that whole, constantly self-destroying and self-regenerating tribe would at last leave him totally indifferent. They bore the faces of the fate of their day, which they were deluded enough to think they determined, but they themselves were at the same time the blind masks of a force that swept across the world. You should not take too much notice of them, that was all. But what was called "governing," the inadmissible desire to be the executor of fate, the temporary face of that most mysterious of all monsters, the state, seemed to him later, much later, despicable.

At exactly a quarter to six the dog lifted its head and Arnold Taads put down his book.

"Athos! Come for a walk!"

They left the house and entered the vaulted, dark shade of the wood. The host soon diverged from the path that had caused his former mistress such trouble and turned into a small side track. But with Taads, there was no question of stumbling or falling. Inni had difficulty in keeping up with the bushranger's jacket in front of him. The dog, on the other hand, seemed to know exactly where the walk led. His presence had become invisible and could only be deduced from the quick riffle of dead leaves somewhere ahead. "Sartre," said the gray wavy hair, the smallish skull, the chamois jacket, the corduroy trousers, and the Russia-leather boots in front of him, "Sartre says we should draw the ultimate conclusion from the fact that God does not exist. Do you believe in God?"

"No," Inni called out. After all, the man had said that on their impending visit to his aunt he did not want to go to church.

"Since when don't you?" asked the pine trees and the bramble bushes.

He knew exactly when it had been, but whether he would say so he did not know. It had had something to do with wine and blood, real wine and real blood, and you just try to explain that. The best thing would, of course, be to say that the little faith he had ever possessed had simply poured out of him like oil out of a defective engine. Up to the age of twelve his upbringing had hardly been

FOR THE BEST LITERATURE, LOOK FOR THE 

☐ **A SPORT OF NATURE**
Nadine Gordimer

Hillela, Nadine Gordimer's "sport of nature," is seductive and intuitively gifted at life. Casting herself adrift from her family at seventeen, she lives among political exiles on an East African beach, marries a black revolutionary, and ultimately plays a heroic role in the overthrow of apartheid.
354 pages *ISBN: 0-14-008470-3*

☐ **THE COUNTERLIFE**
Philip Roth

By far Philip Roth's most radical work of fiction, *The Counterlife* is a book of conflicting perspectives and points of view about people living out dreams of renewal and escape. Illuminating these lives is the skeptical, enveloping intelligence of the novelist Nathan Zuckerman, who calculates the price and examines the results of his characters' struggles for a change of personal fortune.
372 pages *ISBN: 0-14-009769-4*

☐ **THE MONKEY'S WRENCH**
Primo Levi

Through the mesmerizing tales told by two characters—one, a construction worker/philosopher who has built towers and bridges in India and Alaska; the other, a writer/chemist, rigger of words and molecules—Primo Levi celebrates the joys of work and the art of storytelling.
174 pages *ISBN: 0-14-010357-0*

☐ **IRONWEED**
William Kennedy

"Riding up the winding road of Saint Agnes Cemetery in the back of the rattling old truck, Francis Phelan became aware that the dead, even more than the living, settled down in neighborhoods." So begins William Kennedy's Pulitzer-Prize winning novel about an ex-ballplayer, part-time gravedigger, and full-time drunk, whose return to the haunts of his youth arouses the ghosts of his past and present. *228 pages* *ISBN: 0-14-007020-6*

☐ **THE COMEDIANS**
Graham Greene

Set in Haiti under Duvalier's dictatorship, *The Comedians* is a story about the committed and the uncommitted. Actors with no control over their destiny, they play their parts in the foreground; experience love affairs rather than love; have enthusiasms but not faith; and if they die, they die like Mr. Jones, by accident.
288 pages *ISBN: 0-14-002766-1*

Catholic, after all. The humiliating seed of which others have to bear the excessive growth had been sown too late for it to take root properly. He had been christened, but his parents could not marry in church because his father was divorced. A later marriage of his mother to a devout Catholic had brought him face to face with this religion, but only its theatrical, external aspects had fascinated him. The singing, the incense, and the colors had appealed to him so much that he would not have minded entering the monastery even without believing.

Another thing that attracted him about the Catholic faith was that others *did* believe in it. At boarding school he had served as altar boy every morning at six o'clock for the half-demented Father Romualdus, who was too old to teach and was only allowed to do a bit of surveillance. To the belching old man at the altar it really was true that when he whispered *hic est enim Calix Sanguinis mei*, the small measure of red wine changed into blood, became blood, *mysterium fidei*—the blood, at that, of someone who had been dead for almost two thousand years and which the old, brocade-clad man in front of him, who had to hold on to the edge of the altar, would presently drink "in remembrance of Me." It was blood of which Inni would help remove the last traces by pouring a cruet of water into the gold chalice raised to him by trembling, speckled old hands and in which a few drops of divine blood, human blood, had remained behind. Inni had found this unspeakably mysterious, but that was no reason to believe in it. If the man with whom he busied himself on those dark cold mornings and who moved this way and that in front of the little slaughter table like a gold-stitched toad believed in it, then it was true, even if only in that half-softened brain which at times tended to muddle up the Latin phrases in ways so unacceptable that Inni, in his sharp boy's voice, had to lead the speaker back to theologically more correct sequences.

But it was not only that. It was also the notion of sacrifice, of offering. There they were, totally unobserved in their strange twosomeness of sixteen and well over eighty, busy with mysterious, antique rituals that gave Inni a feeling of sinking far back into time. He felt that he was no longer imprisoned in this wretched neo-Gothic squalor but that he had arrived in the landscapes of ancient Greece, the world of Homer, whose secrets they unraveled every day in class, or at the sacrificial offering of live animals by the Jews to the God with the terrible voice who resided above the scorching deserts. This was the God of Vengeance, the God of the Burning Bush and the wife of Lot, a God who, thought Inni, was surrounded by a cosmos of emptiness and fear and punishment for those who believed in him. What they were doing there, Father Romualdus and he, had to do with the Minotaur, with divine offerings and mysteries, with the Sibyls, with fate and destiny. It was a very small bullfight for two men, from which the bull was absent yet had a wound from which the blood was being drunk—a mystery accompanied by low whisperings in Latin.

Once, and then for good, the spell had been broken. As the chalice was being lifted to where, high above the church, the sun would soon trace its course, the old man suddenly began to tremble. Inni would never forget the scream that followed, never. The raised hands let go of the chalice. The wine, the blood, poured all over his chasuble, and the cloth was torn from the altar in one haul by the monk's clawing hands, dragging candles, host, and paten with it. A scream as of a huge wounded animal bounced back from the stone walls. The man tugged at his chasuble as though he was trying to tear it asunder, and then, still screaming, he slowly began to fall. His head hit the chalice and started to bleed. When he was already dead, he still went on bleeding, red and red mingled on the islands of shiny silk amid the gold brocade, and it was no longer clear which was which—the wine had become blood, the blood wine.

The absent dog, the silence of the woods, the soundless footsteps of Old Shatterhand, and his own townish rustle were still waiting for an answer.

"I don't know. Perhaps I never did believe," he shouted ahead. The scornful laugh of a magpie replied. And suddenly the whole wood was full of church fathers, inquisitors, martyrs, confessors, agnostics, heathens, philosophers, bleaters, and brayers. Theological arguments flew all around. Two finches were discussing the Council of Trent, a cuckoo underlined the Summa Theologica, a woodpecker endorsed the thirty-one articles, and sparrows condemned Hus to the stake once again. Spinoza the heron, Calvin the crow, the incomprehensible cooing of the Spanish mystics, the chirping, twittering, gurgling, and clucking birds of field and woodland celebrated the two bloody millennia of church history, from the first swimming fishes scratched on the dark walls of the catacombs to the spirit that had singed Saint Paul in the guise of an inhabitant of Nagasaki, from the perplexity of the men of Emmaus to the infallible vicar occupying the See of the Fisherman. Oceans of that same human blood had been shed since then, and millions of times that same body had been consumed. Not an hour, not a day went by without this being done, at the North Pole, in Burma, Tokyo, and Namibia (oh, Zita), even at the moment when these two unbelievers were walking here under the linden, one with his head full of Sartre, the other with his head full of nothing.

They came to a clearing. Bumblebees buzzed in and out of the purple-brown flowers of the deadly nightshade. Everything quivered and rustled.

"Athos! Come here!"

The dog appeared out of nowhere and lay down at the feet of his master, who posted himself in the middle of the clearing like a field preacher, carrying the late sunlight on his chamois shoulders. Arnold Taads's voice filled the entire wood as if it were an element like water or fire.

"I know exactly at what moment I ceased to believe in God. I have always been a good skier. Before the war I was champion of the Netherlands a couple of times. That may not sound like much, but I was the best, nevertheless, and of course these championships were not won in the Netherlands but in the mountains. Have you ever seen mountains?"

Inni shook his head.

"Then you have not lived yet. Mountains are God's majesty on earth. At least, so I thought. A skier all alone, high up in the mountains, is different from other people. There are only two things, he and nature. He is on a par with the rest of the world, do you understand?"

Inni nodded.

"I have never cared much for people. Most of them are cowards, conformists, muddleheads, moneygrubbers, and they infect each other. Up there you are not bothered by any of that. Nature is pure, like the animals. I feel more love for this dog than for all people put together. Animals are straight, and good for them! When the war was over and we could at last see what exactly had been going on—treason, hunger, murder, and annihilation, all of it done by men—then I really did despise mankind. Not every individual, but the sort that crawls murdering, lying, and frightened towards his own death. Animals are straight, animals don't have slogans, they don't die for someone else, and they don't die for more than their due, either. In our modern society of weaklings the pecking order is a much maligned concept, but it always worked splendidly until man arrived on the evolutionary scene. So, I had had enough of it. I gave up my job as a notary, I burnt all my boats behind me, I broke with my wife—ah, wonderful, wonderful!—and I went to Canada. There I became a fire warden in the Rocky Mountains. For months on end I sat on a high mountaintop. Below me, a landscape of endless forests stretched out in all directions. I sat there peering at it. If I saw smoke, I had to raise the alarm. Provisions were brought to me by plane. Once a week they dropped a sack of food, newspapers, and mail on the patch of ground beside my cabin. For six months I stayed there alone with my dog and my friend the radio, not for the sake of the stupid honky-tonk garbage you hear on it but for the nightly conversations with other men at other posts. Two fingers of whiskey I allowed myself, two a day"—he raised two joined fingers horizontally to Inni—"never more. If I had once taken more, I would have gone crazy. Then they would have had to haul a raving madman down the mountain. I wrote it all down."

Inni had never been in the mountains, but that was no reason for not now having a vision of this man who was standing here before him—in a white, icy world. Four Swiss picture postcards enclosed the small log cabin. The man was wearing the same chamois jacket as now, the dog lay asleep at his feet, it was time for his whiskey, and there was a gale howling around the cabin. The picture postcards were angry. From the radio came the crackles and groans of a distant, despised world. The man stood up, went to a cupboard, and took out the whiskey bottle and a glass. (He had looked at a clock before doing so.) Then he held two fingers horizontally one above the other beside the glass on the table—no, a millimeter above the table because the thickness of the bottom of the glass had to be taken into account—and poured. Glug-glug. Not until some time later did he take a sip. A taste of smoke and hazelnut.

"And one day I thought: a landscape which, let us say, by its objective majesty evokes the idea of God can, of course, equally well evoke his absence. God was created after the image and likeness of men. This is what everyone grasps in the end, except people who never grasp anything. But I despise people, including"—here was a slight raising of the tone, which gave the word a clipped independence, so that it hovered briefly, in isolation and pregnant with meaning, in the open space between them—"myself, of course. I detest myself. But however much I love dogs and mountains, I was nevertheless unable to imagine God in the shape of a dog or a mountain. And so the idea of God vanished from my life, like a skier going down a slope into the valley. Can you picture it? Seen from a distance the tiny human figure looks black. It writes itself like calligraphy on the white sheet of snow. A long, graceful movement, a mysterious, illegible letter being written, something that is there and is suddenly no longer there. It is lost from sight. It wrote itself and left nothing behind. For the first time I was alone in the world, but I would not miss Him. God sounds like an answer—that is what is most pernicious about the word. It has so often been used as an answer. He should have had a name that sounded like a question. I never asked to be alone in the world, but then, nobody does. Do you ever think about these things?"

Inni knew already that the inquiring tone in which the sentence was uttered did not imply a question but a command. His dossier was being compiled, and he was being measured. Between him and this man deeds had to be drawn up. But what should he say? He felt a strange indifference. The warmth, the half-hidden colors of flowers, the gently swaying lime trees above him, all these things happening at once, the whole fabric of sensory perceptions, the dog stretching himself and hesitantly walking a little way farther to a spot where there was still sun, this whole new life which had started only that afternoon but seemed to have lasted so long already, the hammering voice continuously talking about himself, the whiskey he had been given to drink—all this gave him a feeling of not being. So much was happening, he could easily be dispensed with. He was the vessel that was filling up. If he were to speak now, all these new, precious sensations would pour out of him. He heard every word the man said, but what exactly was it all about? "Do you ever think about these things?" What is thinking? He had never seen God going down a slope like a skier. God was a wine stain on a chasuble, the blood of an old man on an icy-cold freestone altar step. But you did not say such things.

"No, never," he said.

"Why not?"

"It does not occupy me."

"I see."

He realized that a reply of a more cosmic aspect was being expected of him, but he did not have one.

"Do you know anything about existentialism?"

You bet he did. Three debating evenings they had devoted to it, in his last year at boarding school. Sartre, free choice, Juliette Greco, candlelit cellars, black pullovers, boys who had been to Paris and had come home with Gauloises, which you could not get in the Netherlands, cold Camembert, and French bread, of which those same friends said it could not compare with real French bread because that was much crisper. Despair and nausea had had something to do with it, too. Man had been thrown into the world. It had always made him think of Icarus and those other great tumblers, Ixion, Phaeton, Tantalus—all those jumpers without parachutes from a world of gods and heroes who interested him far more than those strange abstractions of which he could form no visual image. A meaningless world into which you were thrown, an existence that signified nothing except by virtue of what you made it signify. It still smacked of church. It had a suspect, musty odor of martyrdom. Most of all, thought Inni, it found its expression in the taste and the smell of those Gauloises—strong, bitter, unlike anything else—a smell that had something dangerous about it, tobacco that clung to your tongue with small, bitter prickles, the crude billiard-chalk blue packet. You could smoke your fear away with them. But that was a word he would never utter to this man.

"Not much."

What use could this skiing champion have for philosophy? What did he want of the small, squinting scholar whose portrait appeared so regularly in newspapers and magazines these days? Thinking—what was that exactly, anyway? He read a lot, but what he read, and not just that but everything he saw, films and paintings, he translated into feeling. And this feeling, which could not immediately be expressed in words, not yet and maybe never, that formless mass of sentiments, impressions, observations—that was his way of thinking. You could circle around it with words, but there always remained far more that was not expressed than was. And later, too, a certain resentment would take possession of him, toward those people who demanded precise answers, or pretended to be able to give them. It was, on the contrary, the very mystery of everything that was so attractive. You should not want to impose too much order on it. If you did, something would be lost irrevocably. That mysteries can become more mysterious if you think about them with precision and method, he did not yet know. He felt at home in his sentimental chaos. To chart it you had to be an adult, but then you were at once labeled, finished, and in effect already a bit dead.

"I don't mean Christian but atheist existentialism . . ."

Get on your skis! Whiz down a slope in pursuit of your vanished God. Go and sit on a mountaintop. Look about for fires. Go away! Leave me alone!

". . . That goes too far for me, though. The ethical, humanist side of it doesn't appeal to me. It makes man somehow pathetic, a kind of clown groping around in the dark trying to find the exit. That's what I don't like about it. It isn't cruel enough. Do you understand?"

Inni nodded. These were words he understood. Patches of haze, as ungraspable as the dancing flecks of light high up in the trees. How many shades of green were there?

"When Sartre says man has been thrown into the world, he is alone, there is no God, we are responsible for what we are, what we do, I say yes!"

The affirmative echoed around the woods. The dog pricked up his ears. This man has no one to talk to, thought Inni.

"But when he then asks me to be responsible for the world as well, for others, I say no! No. Why should I be? 'When man chooses himself, he chooses all men.' Why? I have not asked for anything. I have nothing to do with the vermin I see around me. I live out my time because I have to, that is all."

And as if to make an immediate start, he turned round in a furious pirouette and disappeared into the woods. The dog had already gone ahead.

Had he been set thinking after all? Then it was obviously infectious. As long as you did not do anything yourself, your life was determined by the people and the things that occurred in it. Their presence set into motion a slow stream of events you had to drag along with you: dead fathers, foreign mothers, boarding schools, guardians, and now also an aunt and a skiing champion. With a certain satisfaction he reflected that once again there had been no need for him to do anything himself. But how was it, then, that while he had the feeling that he had done nothing himself and that everything had only happened *to* him, his life seemed so long? He had already been here for thousands of years, and if he had studied zoology, it would have been millions. Small wonder, with such a past, that you could not remember everything, and yet at the same time it was surprising what you did remember. And stranger still was the equivalence of these recollections, in which the announcement of his father's death was on a par with all kinds of other annexed events, such as Thalassa Thalassa, the Crucifixion, and the burning of the Reichstag. All of it was you, in effect, for although you had not yourself experienced it all, it had woven itself into your life. Ultimately, it was your body that remembered these things for you. Strange chemical processes in your brain had seen to it that you were aware of the Paleozoic, which therefore, somehow or other, had become part of your experience, so that you yourself were connected with unimaginably distant times to which you would belong until you died, by virtue of that same mysterious mechanism. Consequently, your life was stretched out infinitely—that was not to be denied. He suddenly felt very old.

The silence of the man who had just spoken at such length became emphatic. Had he been tried and found wanting?

The woods became sparser and lighter, the trees opened out, and through the last remaining, meager battle formations, he saw a tall shield of light through which they would presently walk and which veiled the purple heath in a dreamy, hazy glow, making everything seem very empty and very still.

He would have liked to pause. Better still he would have liked to lie down, to press his face into those sharp, crumbly plants, his body against the ground, as he so often did when he was alone, because then he felt he could slowly merge with the earth, really get inside it with his knees, his chest, and his chin, with everything that was hard and bony about him. Thus he would not be like a cat lying on a cushion. No, he would be more like the half-silted-up wreckage of a ship. But for that kind of love affair, there was no place on a woodland walk with Arnold Taads. He was convinced that if he slowed down, his name would boom across the heath as if he were a dog.

Or had Taads already forgotten him? He did not look up or back and would probably have been able to walk the same route blindfolded, with the same rhythmic, mechanical movements. A wound-up toy soldier on the march. As they reached the house, the clock struck seven.

Time, Inni learned that day, was the father of all things in Arnold Taads's life. He had divided the empty, dangerous expanse of the day into a number of precisely measured parts, and the boundary posts at the beginning and end of each part determined his day with unrelenting sternness. Had he been older, Inni would have known that the fear that dominated Arnold Taads demanded its tithes in hours, half hours, and quarter hours, randomly applied points of fracture in the invisible element through which we must wade as long as we live. It was as if, in an endless desert, someone had singled out a particular grain of sand and decided that only there could he eat and read. Each of these preappointed grains of sand called forth, with compelling force, its own complementary activity. A mere ten millimeters farther and fate would strike. Someone arriving ten minutes early or late was not welcome. The maniacal second hand turned the first page, played the first note on the piano, or, as now, put a pan of goulash on the stove on the last stroke of seven.

"I cook once a week," said Arnold Taads, "usually a stew. And soup. I make exactly enough, seven portions for myself and one for a guest. If no one comes, Athos gets it."

Inni was pleased he would be eating the dog's portion. He did not care much for dogs, especially when they lived in such suffocating symbiosis with their masters. Quarter past seven struck, and they sat down at the table.

"When we visit your aunt Thérèse next week," said Taads, "you will find it a complete madhouse. Most of the Wintrops have a screw loose, but when it comes to choosing a mate, total lunacy takes over. Mostly they tend to pick someone who is quite normal, and then they drive him insane in the shortest possible time, or else they take someone they don't have to spend any effort on because he is soft in the head already. After I had given your aunt the push, she married an absolute imbecile, with money of course, and she became very unhappy as a result, as you have been able to observe for yourself. A number one neurotic. I am glad I got out in time. She was a beautiful woman in the old days, very attractive, but with a kind of impetuous possessiveness that frightened me. Your whole family frightened me, actually. They have two faults: they never know where to draw the line, and they refuse to suffer. By that I mean this: they deny everything that borders on the unpleasant. They turn away from it. They know sentimentality but not loyalty.

When things get tough, they are off. Your aunt finds it amusing to dump you here on my doorstep, but she should have known better than to pick an ex-notary. We shall concoct a tidy little settlement out of this for you. Why I bother, God knows. Probably out of spite. But you seem to have a certain talent, although I wouldn't know what for."

He ate in the same way that he walked—fast, with mechanical movements. A feeding automaton. If for whatever reason, thought Inni, he suddenly looked sideways, that independent arm, driven by a different authority, would poke the fork into his cheek. Half past seven, clearing the table and making coffee. Quarter to eight, coffee and "my fourth cigarette. The fifth I smoke before I go to bed."

The heavy scent of a Black Beauty wafted through the room.

"What is it like," asked Arnold Taads, "not to have a father?"

This man asked only questions to which there were no answers. So Inni did not reply. Not to have a father was *not* to have something. So there was nothing to say about it.

"Did you ever miss him?"

"No."

"Did you know him?"

"Until I was ten."

"What do you remember of him?"

He thought about his father, but because it was virtually the first time he had ever done so deliberately, he found it difficult. His father used to say "so long" when leaving the house, and once he had hit his mother in Inni's presence, and, as Inni had gathered, on other occasions too, when he was not present. And one night when, woken by the air raid siren, he had rushed down the stairs in a panic, he had surprised his father on the sofa with the nursemaid. From that, in retrospect, somewhat uncomfortable position, he had ordered Inni back to his bedroom. Later his father had married the nursemaid, his mother having disappeared as a result of one of those mysterious maneuvers with which grown-ups bend the world to their will. Inni had stayed with his father and the girl, but in the hunger winter he had been sent to his mother, who lived somewhere in Gelderland. At the end of that winter his father had been killed during the bombing of The Hague. The news had filled Inni with pride. Now he, too, was really part of the war.

He had never seen his father's grave, and when he had begun to take an interest in it, it was no longer there. It had been cleared, someone told him—a very special variant of "cleared away"—and so he had remembered it: his father had been cleared away. In yellowy war photographs he would see a balding man with sharp features, a somber clerk from the late Middle Ages, although his mother had told him he used to dance on top of bar tables, to gypsy music. These were the memories he had of his father, and there was only one conclusion: his father was well and truly dead.

"I don't remember much."

Then Taads again, this time in the disguise of a professor. "Sartre says that if you have no father, you are not burdened with a superego. No father on your back, no bullying regulating factor in your life. Nothing to rebel against or to hate or to measure your conduct against."

I don't know about that, thought Inni. If it meant that he was alone in the world, it was correct. That was what he himself felt, too, and it suited him splendidly. Other people, like the man facing him now, had to be kept at a distance. And they should not talk too much about him either. As long as they talked about themselves, or about his relations, none of whom he knew anyway, it was fine. He had twice been expelled from boarding school because he "did not fit in with the other boys," he "did not join in," he "had a perfidious influence on the other students." They hated him—that would have been a more accurate way of putting it. They had put litanies of hatred in his bed ("Sour lemon, pray for us"), but it had left him strangely unmoved. Those boys were different. On visiting days they were surrounded by families, fathers in brown suits and mothers in floral-print dresses. He had nothing to do with them, any more than with this man here who had come straying into his life. He refused to allow them in, that was what it boiled down to. It was just as if everything happened in a film. He might be sitting in the audience following the action attentively, certainly if the actors were as fascinating as this one, but really to be part of it was impossible. He remained, even when he felt sympathy for the actor, an onlooker. If you kept silent, the stories would come all by themselves.

And come they did.

In that silent room, the story of his family was unfolded, as in a recitative according to the gospel of Arnold Taads. There was no place in this devastating account for the light relief of an aria. Instead, there came every now and again, welling up from an abyss of doom and sorrow, the deep sigh of the dog, which the anonymous composer had interpolated in masterly fashion; for exactly in the brief interval after the description of yet another Wintrop folly, aberration, or monstrous deed, the dog, with a perfect sense of timing, let a thrust of air escape from the subterranean labyrinths to which he was apparently connected.

Would they rehearse? wondered Inni. Dogs do not live all that long, and with one extra portion of goulash a week they clearly did not expect too many visitors. The only possible answer was that these lectures, sermons, recitatives, were also delivered in solitude, with the dog doing duty as continuo, punctuation, and emphasis. Light, air—this talented animal had learned to fill the invisible airstream that envelops us and partly flows through us, with affects and affirmations. He had discovered the meaning of destiny and disgust, not leaving them hanging in the indifferent surrounding air, prey to the destructive metronomics of the mantelpiece clock. On the contrary he filled the air in artistic convolution with his one-eyed master, with something that was at the same time the echo of what had just been uttered and a lighter, more vicious whiplash forcing the soloist to maintain the tension thus far achieved.

This tension, Inni was to learn, was a negative force. He did not appreciate it immediately, though that first evening already contained the seed of his friendship with Arnold Taads. One of his characteristics—and this, too, he did not know at the time, because whatever his own views on the matter, he had simply not yet lived long enough—was that he could never turn his back on anyone in whom he had once become interested. Often these were what the outside world, the world of all other people combined, would call "odd fish," people that seemed totally incongruous with Inni's sarcastic or urbane style. "There's another one from Inni's sewer, madhouse, collection, underworld. . . . Who on earth did I see you with at Schiphol yesterday? . . . How can you possibly spend an evening with *her*? . . . Are you still seeing that same girl?"

But all that came later.

Now it was Arnold Taads, a man whose relations with the world had been unsuccessful and who therefore pushed the world away from himself in high-pitched, sharp tones as if he were still its master. If this messenger of renunciation had been the fifth Evangelist, he would have had a seagull as his symbol, a solitary gray shape on a rock, standing out against the darker shades of an ominous sky. Inni had seen them in nature films, stalked by telephoto lenses. How they suddenly threw their beaks wide open, let out a piercing cry of rage and warning, and with vigorous wingbeats, swept into the sky, where still alone, they sailed away on an invisible, gently heaving airstream. And then again, at intervals those cries, as if something had to be slashed, demolished.

The clock struck. The man and the dog stood up.

"I'll take you to the bus stop," said Arnold Taads.

From a stand in the hall he took a wooden, umbrellalike object covered with a kind of shiny parchment.

"This is a parong," he said. Indeed, no sooner were they outside than the rain was making loud tapping noises on the stretched surface. Everything fit. As they walked down the garden path, Inni looked back at the house, and even more than when they were inside, he was conscious of the fierce loneliness to which this man had condemned himself. There are many different forms of suffering, and although Inni, in retrospect, must have had his fair share of unhappiness, it is nevertheless rare for the raw state of suffering to be revealed to someone of his age as clearly as happened now. Suffering, not as an event, but as a deliberately sought, irrevocable punishment. Irrevocable because no other people were involved in it, because this man who was marching along beside him so buoyantly and robustly, like an athlete who has beaten the world record, appeared to suffer from himself, in himself. Without being able to define it at the time, Inni knew he was here confronted with the smell of death, a realm from which one cannot return if, perhaps by accident or simply through inattention, one has strayed into it.

He was relieved when the bus, exactly on time, drove off. Arnold Taads and his dog had already vanished into the night, the rain, the woods.

The bus, the train, the long walk through the tree-lined roads of Hilversum, along which the villas stood like dark tombs in their gardens, and sultry, heavy scents of flowers after rain—among all this sweetness was a strange taste of farewell. To what exactly he did not yet know, but that a farewell had to be said, was certain.

That night he did not dream of Arnold Taads because he could not sleep. Yet the vision he had, in which Taads played a part, was more like a dream than anything else. His host was sitting opposite him, exactly as he had done in reality that evening. He was undoubtedly the same man who had taken him to the bus stop a few hours earlier, the man with the two skins and the one eye, a person who had appeared in his life as an instrument of fate. Inni could never refrain from attaching to the word *appear* that special significance that, for Catholics, it has had since Fatima and Lourdes. Nor could it be denied that Arnold Taads was more of an apparition than anything else, and a seated one at that, a variant never mentioned with reference to the Virgin Mother. The other paraphernalia were all there. From the standard lamp poured a constant nimbus of electrified sanctity around the battered face. The only thing that did not really fit was that this sanctity was unwilling to impart itself to the actual face, which with its many incongruities, appeared to preclude serenity. This was a saint broken in two, who had already suffered so much that he was allowed to bathe in this unearthly glow but whose face still showed so many traces of other, darker worlds that you could not even be sure you were not dealing with a deceptive manifestation of the devil. And now a pimple, lump, wart—he wasn't sure exactly what—some kind of unevenness, an imperfection of the skin, had become noticeable, and the heavenly lamplight carved more sharply the two deep, scornful, tormented furrows running from the sides of the nose to the mouth. Even more than the eyes, because even the blind, directionless eye joined in and filled at least half of the geometric room with unseen torments, he remembered in the half-sleep of that night those two furrows that, like thin puppet strings, controlled the corners of the mouth, making them rise and fall independently of each other. With the associated story Inni was to regale his friends until well into old age, though never without feeling a knife-thrust of guilt toward the dead man he was betraying, who had, in fact, perished through the impact of that story.

"I can't go back to the Rocky Mountains," said Arnold Taads. "Too old. They don't want me any more. That is why I go to a lonely valley in the Swiss Alps every year. You probably can't form a mental picture of it, and I shan't tell you where it is. I never do. I rent a deserted farmhouse that the owners use only in the summer. People, even those people, have become soft, pampered. Nobody can be alone anymore, and no one wants to be alone. They refuse to face the winter and the loneliness up there. As soon as the first snow falls, the valley becomes totally isolated. You can only get there on skis."

"What about food?" asked Inni.

"I go down to fetch it once every two weeks. I don't need much. You can live on very little, but nobody knows that these days. In any case I can't carry much on my back, because it is a six-hour trip."

Inni nodded. Six hours! "How am I to imagine that?" he asked.

Arnold Taads screwed up one eye into something that looked like an obscene wink which lasted for several minutes.

"Like this," he said. "Stand beside me." (This was to become Inni's celebrated mime number on skis.) "We're going up, we're climbing. Sharp east wind. Unpleasant. Remember, you're carrying a rucksack on your back. It's heavy. There's fourteen days' food in it, for the dog as well. We have another four hours to go. Look at me."

The eye was still screwed up.

"You've still got your eye open. I can see with only one eye. The blind eye is closed now. Shut your right eye. That distorts the perspective, and it eliminates a good thirty percent of normal vision. Look. Quite dangerous on a trip like this. Try it out."

Part of the right half of the room was cut off.

"If I go too fast, there is always a risk of something—a stone, a branch, an obstacle that I don't see."

"And then?"

Arnold Taads had sat down again. Inni found it difficult to imagine that the reopened, gleaming eye was really a hole which distorted the world so that the left eye had to fight a double battle to guard its owner against a fatal fall in the snow or on the ice.

"Then I might fall and break my leg. In theory, but it is possible."

The east wind blew through the room. The afternoon sun reflected the blinding light of the glacier in his one eye. No houses anywhere, no people. The world as it had always been, without interference. In the vast, white space lay a small figure, the skis jutting out crosswise like the first sticks of a campfire. A doll's leg twisted the wrong way round.

"And what will you do then?"

Freeze to death of course, he thought, but for the answer that came he was unprepared.

"Then I give the Alpine distress signal." And without any warning his host bellowed "Hilfe!" raised his hand in adjuration as if to summon the same cruel silence to the room as reigned in that distant fateful valley, and then silently but with open mouth counted up to three and called out again "Hilfe!" one, two, three, "Hilfe!" His face turned purple in the process, and the glass eye looked as if it was about to pop out of its socket, through the terrible force of the shout.

Inni looked at the contorted, distressed carnival mask in front of him. Never before had he seen such a defenseless face. He felt embarrassment and pity—the embarrassment that he would always feel in the presence of someone else's intimate actions and the pity for a man who has been lying with a broken leg in a deserted valley for years and has no one to tell it to.

"I will keep on doing that, three times in a row, counting up to three each time until I have no strength left. Sound carries a long way in the mountains."

"But if there is no one there to hear?"

"Then the sound does not exist. Only I hear it. But it is not intended for me. If that sound does not reach the stranger for whom it is intended, it does not exist. And it won't take long before I shall not exist any more, either. You freeze, you become drowsy, you don't call out any more, you die."

Of course the dog did not understand these words, but the decisive tone born out of future disaster could not fail to produce an effect. Athos got up, whimpered softly, and shook himself as if to throw something off.

"By the time they start looking for me, Athos will already be dead," said Taads. "That is what troubles me most of all. My own death is a calculated risk, and there ought to be a way to safeguard Athos from that. But there isn't."

It was the first time that someone had told Inni Wintrop the precise details of his death, even though it would be years before it occurred.

Opulence, not wealth, was the word to describe the interior of his aunt's spacious villa. Chesterfields, seventeenth-century cupboards, paintings of the Dutch school, a voluptuous Renaissance ivory crucifix, entire families of Sèvres and Limoges, Persian carpets, servants—he was being wrapped up in it all as in a warm shawl.

"How people can live among the shit of the past is a mystery to me," said Taads when they were alone for a moment. "Everything is tainted. Everything has already been admired by others. Antique stinks. Hundreds of eyes that have rotted away long ago have looked at it. You can tolerate it only if you have a junkyard inside yourself as well."

Inni did not reply. If this was so contemptible, there must be something wrong with him too. He thought it was all blissfully comfortable, and at the same time it expressed power and therefore distance from the world outside.

"Thérèse, a bourgeois is being born this afternoon," said Taads as his aunt entered the room. "And you are standing by the cradle. Just look at the delighted face of your new nephew. He recognizes his natural surroundings. Watch the easy grace with which he is immediately turning into a Wintrop."

Arnold Taads's entry had been impressive enough. Even when formulating it to himself, Inni thought it sounded exaggerated. But that afternoon he had discovered, for once not judging by his own example, that a distance can exist between people which expresses such a terrible otherness that anyone witnessing it will almost die of melancholy. Everyone knows these things, but no one has always known them—upright-walking creatures of the same species, who moreover use the same language to make it clear to each other that there is an unbridgeable chasm between them. A fool—this Inni could see, too—had arranged this lunch. The three plates from which they were to eat—the "uncle" had not yet manifested himself—were practically engulfed by an overabundance of cold meats. My God, how many ways are there to mess about with the corpses of animals. Smoked, boiled, roasted, in aspic, blood red, black and white checkered, fatty pink, murky white, marbled, pressed, ground, sliced. Thus death lay displayed on the blue-patterned Meissen. Not even a whole school could have eaten all that. Taads, who looked much smaller in this house, stood behind the chair assigned to him and surveyed the battlefield. Filtered sunlight caressed the white, the yellow, the soft, the hard, and the blue-veined cheeses.

"This is a Brabant lunch," said his aunt. She raised her face towards Taads, full of anticipation. It was for him she had put on this display. Taads remained silent. The single eye scanned the table mercilessly, relentlessly. At last the verdict came, a whiplash. "I say, Thérèse, haven't you got any ham?"

His aunt reeled under the blow. Red blotches rushed to her face. She staggered out of the room, and from the hall they heard a long, smothered wail that ran up the stairs at a gallop and vanished behind the slam of a door.

"This is a Brabant lunch," Taads said with satisfaction as he sat down. "Revolting late-Burgundian affectation. Those wealthy textile farmers still seem to think they are the heirs of the Burgundian court. This is the Bavaria of the Netherlands, my boy. A Calvinist doesn't belong here."

"I thought you were a Catholic, too," said Inni.

"North of the great rivers, all Dutchmen are Calvinists. We don't believe in too much, too long, or too dear. If these people here had their way, you'd be sitting at the table until three o'clock."

There was a tap on the door. A girl came in with a dish of ham that she put down in front of Taads.

"Will this be all right, sir?"

She was tall and slender, with big breasts and a crooked comedian's face in which green eyes could barely control their laughter. She spoke with a broad Brabant accent.

Inni fell in love with her. Later (the dreadful, mischievous later that seemed to rule over everything and in which all experiences were to be filed as in a court of law), he would define those sudden, senseless infatuations: "The physical element has almost nothing to do with it. At most it helps to make you aware of it a little sooner. It is the knowledge, instinctive, sudden, and sure, that somebody is okay."

"Okay?"

"Yes, that she is in tune with herself. I can't fall for someone who is not in tune with herself. And the other keystone—it is a structure after all—is that you know she has something for you."

"Has something for you?"

"Yes. That if the time and the place are right, there is a logic in the encounter."

Logic. The very word would make any lover run a mile. But that was just it. It had to be entirely logical, going to bed with such a person. You knew it would happen because it had to happen. The only thing left to be done was to inform the other person. That was the seduction. The certainty of the outcome was a great help. That, and the strange contradiction that the bed bit was not the main thing at all. This you began to see more clearly when, on occasion, you yourself were the other person. What mattered was whether you were in tune. But the longing, the quivering, that odd, desperate feeling, always the same, which he experienced now at this table, watching her walk so straight and hearing her say that one sentence with that deliciously soft lilt while she glanced at him briefly with her green mocking eyes that laughed at "that old fool with his glass eye and that skinny young one with his funny look as if he couldn't keep his eyes off you"—that had to be there first. Only then came the "verification," a question of adoration, of woman worship. He had been declared mad by his friends as he was off on one of his missions again, flying to the other end of the world merely to follow a line, a thought that someone had left in him and that he had to verify at all costs. Was it so or was it not so? Would he have a chance, with that person, of a life that, if he chose to take it, would become a reality? That was the point. The search was a labor of love, but he could not explain this to anyone.

"And if you're not in tune?"

No. Quite clearly, no one understood anything about it except the women themselves. And then you were in tune.

His aunt did not appear again, and Taads's merciless clock struck here, too. Between three and four he had his snooze, even had he been at Nova Zembla. Inni walked aimlessly about the house and after much hesitation opened the kitchen door. The girl was sitting by a large table, polishing silver.

"Hello," said Inni.

She did not reply, but smiled, unless it was mockery. "What's your name?" she asked.

"Inni."

She exploded with laughter. Her breasts shook. He was consumed by desire. He went up to her and put his hand on her head.

"Hoho," she said, but sat very still until she suddenly picked up a large, freshly polished spoon and held it up with the convex side toward him. Everything he hated in his face was magnified, elongated, emphasized.

"I'm Petra," she said. On this rock, this soft, round rock, he thought later, he had built his church. For there was no doubt about it—on that day women had become his religion, the center, the essence of everything, the great cartwheel on which the world turned.

"What sign are you?"

"Leo." And before she could say anything, he added quickly: "My number is one, my metal gold, my star the sun. And my profession is either king or banker."

"Oy-oy," she said, and put his hand on the table amid the silver. "Shall I show you the village?"

They walked among the Saturday afternoon bustle in the village street. People kept greeting them, and inquisitive glances were cast at him.

"Where are we going?"

"To the woods. But you mustn't tell your aunt."

In the woods it was quiet and cool. They both stuck out their hand at the same moment and walked on holding hands under the tall trees. So simple it would never be again. The leaves, the trees, the lofty beams of mysterious light in the half-dark—everything contributed.

They lay down and he kissed her breasts and her hair, and she held him very close to her and stroked the back of his neck. With a voice that came from beside his face, she told him about her life. She still had her father and mother, and she had been to domestic science school, and she had eight brothers and sisters, and she preferred to work for his aunt rather than at the factory, and her fiancé was a volunteer in Korea, and when he came back in two weeks' time, they were going to get married.

Then she turned around, a girl transformed into a cloud of infinite tenderness. He was no longer able to see what she was doing, but he could feel how she ran cool fingers over his belly, a trail followed by equally cool lips, continually interrupted by tiny, warm licks of her tongue. He raised his head to look at her. She was lying half on top of him. Of her head he saw only the mass of dark hair.

Her right hand, the hand that an hour earlier had placed a dish of ham before Arnold Taads, stood firmly braced among the moss and the dead, softly creaking beech leaves. For the first time he felt that blend of love, longing, and emotion for which he would from now on have to search all his life. Her head moved gently. He had a feeling as though he were being drunk from, and then he no longer had any feeling or thought. He saw only the black hair and the firm hand in the moss, detached from everything. And then he spilled out into her mouth, at the same time suddenly grabbing her hair and, as she said later, hurting her.

For a while they lay without moving. Then she raised her head and, still with that hand as a pivot, swung a quarter turn toward him. In her eyes there was still a trace of mockery, but mingled now with triumph and tenderness. She smiled, opened her mouth briefly so that he saw his white seed on her pink tongue, rolled her eyes as though imitating a film star, and swallowed. Then she turned around altogether, stretched herself headlong on top of him, kissed him full on the mouth, and said, "Come on, let's go."

They walked back in silence. By the first houses of the village she asked him if he would go home a little after her. Leaning against a wall, he watched her as she slowly, rockingly, walked away from him, not looking back once. When he arrived home, he did not see her anywhere.

Dinner was a greater catastrophe than lunch. The uncle who had hitherto existed only in name had become flesh and was sitting at the head of the table, wrapped in massive drunkenness. Taads looked with disdain at the army of crystal wine glasses by his plate, and Inni's aunt was in such a state of agitation that Inni feared she would not last the evening. The fourth man at the table was addressed as Reverend Uncle by the uncle. He was wearing a purple sash, purple buttons on his cassock, and a purple skull cap. "Monsignor Terruwe is private chamberlain to the Pope," his aunt had told him, but he had had no idea how to imagine such a person. The man had a long, exceedingly white face with mud-colored eyes. He was a professor at the theological academy in Rome. During grace before the meal, which he said in a slow and rasping voice, Inni saw him looking at Taads, who had not crossed himself, as if he were setting eyes on a rare reptile for the first time.

The hors d'oeuvre consisted of calf's tongue in a green sauce. His aunt tinkled a little bell. His heart pounded. The girl entered. Her gait had something of a dance, and he noticed that the priest followed her all around the room with his eyes. When she bent forward to pour out the wine, they both saw the high start of her breasts. Their eyes met, and the priest cast his down. Inni hoped she would look at him, that the mockery of those green eyes would briefly flutter over him in confirmation of what had happened that afternoon—that he and no one else had caressed those now concealed breasts at which the mud-colored eyes were looking so covetously. But nothing happened. She filled his glass last, that same small, strong hand holding the bottle of Meursault in its grip. The wine poured golden yellow into the glass.

"To our newly found nephew," said the uncle.

They raised their glasses to him and drank, a strange group of solid shadows that had suddenly somehow become connected with him.

"You have left the Mother Church, Mr. Taads?" asked the chamberlain.

Arnold Taads stared at him and said at last: "Let us try to avoid an argument. What I have to say on the subject would sound most discourteous to your ears."

"My ears are but human ears. It is God's ears you might offend."

Taads said nothing. Inni tried to imagine it. God's ears. Who knows, God might be nothing but ear, a gigantic marble ear floating through space. But God did not exist. The Pope did, that was sure, and this strangely birdlike man was his private chamberlain.

But what was that? If he was so private, no one would know about him. Maybe he was the lord of the private chamber. A secret room in the Vatican where the white, equally birdlike figure of Pius XII resided and to which this man had access, white heron and hooded crow. What would they talk about? Secretive whisperings in Italian, but what about? Perhaps he was the Pope's father confessor. Could a pope sin? He remembered his own sessions in endless sequences in sour-smelling confessionals, the whispered exchanges, the foul male smell in which there floated words like unchastity, repentance, and forgiveness, and his own voice in the repulsive intimacy of the wooden seat. "Alone or with others . . . Sixth Commandment . . . penitence."

"But forgive me my curiosity, Mr. Taads."

Inni saw the ski champion's single eye narrowing.

"I forgive you everything," he said, "but even if I had believed in God, I would have left your church. An institution that is based on suffering and death can never bode any good."

"You mean the sacrificial death of the Son of God?"

"The communists are busy surrounding us," said the uncle. "When they come, our number will be up first."

Arnold Taads reflected. "Monsignor," he said, leaving a pause after *Mon*, so that the full force of the title remained briefly suspended around the priest, like a halo. "God does not exist and therefore he has no son. All religions provide the wrong answer to the same question: why are we on this earth?"

"We are on this earth in order to serve God and thereby to attain heaven," said the uncle as if someone had pressed a button. The big breasts reappeared and poured small glasses of sercial to accompany the consommé.

"I understand you are a professor of theology," Taads continued, "and so this is a very childish conversation. You are filled up to your dog collar with dogma and scholasticism. You know all the arguments to prove the existence of God, and all the counter arguments. You have constructed an entire system on the gruesome symbol of the cross. Your religion still feeds on that one sado-masochistic seance that may never really have taken place. It was the militaristic organization of the Roman Empire that gave this strange cult, with its peculiar mixture of pagan idolatry and good intentions, a chance to develop. The Western thirst for expansion and colonialism enabled it to spread, and the Church that you call a mother has more often been a murderer, usually a tyrant, and always a bully."

"And you have a better answer?"

"I have no answer."

"What is your view of the mystics?"

"Mysticism has nothing to do with any particular religion. Mystics are almost always regarded with suspicion by the official churches. It is a rare opportunity for man to lose himself. If there ever comes a time when there are no longer any religions, there will still be mystics. Mysticism is a faculty of the soul, not of a system. Or did you think that nothingness is not a mystical concept?"

"So you believe in nothingness."

Taads groaned. "You can't believe in nothingness. You can't attach a system to the nonexistence of everything."

"The nonexistence of everything." The chamberlain savored this brief phrase on his tongue. Suddenly he raised his hand. "This hand is real, wouldn't you think?"

"To look at it, yes."

"So it is not nonexistent. And if this plate is the world—let us assume for a moment that it is—then that is not nonexistent either."

"One day," said Taads, "you and I, your hand and this plate and this bottle of Haut Brion and all the rest of the world will no longer exist. Then even our deaths will not exist and everybody else's death will not exist and therefore at the same time all memory will be nonexistent. Then we shall never have existed. That is what I mean."

"And you can live with that?"

"That wasn't the question." For the first time that day Inni saw Taads smile. Some of the grayness drifted away from his face. "I can live perfectly with that. Not always, but usually. Stones, plants, stars—everything lives with that. I am, ah, a colleague of everything that exists. So are you for that matter."

"I beg your pardon?"

"I am, we all are, colleagues of the universe. If you take the line that the human measure means nothing and that nothing is in fact smaller or bigger than anything else, then all of us, people and things, share the same fate. We have had a beginning and we shall have an end, and between the two we exist, the universe as well as a geranium. The universe will exist a little bit longer than you, but this small difference does not make you differ essentially from each other."

"And death?"

"I have not the faintest idea what that is. Have you?"

At this point the dinner party took a strange turn. Inni's aunt burst into tears. Whether it was because of what Taads had just said was not clear, but the consequences were not long in coming. In the silence, punctuated by violent sobs, Arnold Taads's commanding voice boomed forth.

"Thérèse, don't make such an exhibition of yourself."

At this, the sobbing changed into a kind of wailing in which, with some difficulty, the words "never loved me" could be distinguished. As if he were not really there but was suspended from the ceiling, infinitely high up and far away, Inni saw Petra entering the room, taking his aunt in her arms, and leading her away like a half-witted child. At the same time the uncle rose. His huge bulk stumbled toward Taads. Blood turned the patrician neck below the white hair to dark red. Monsignor Terruwe had also risen from his seat and was traveling along a course between Taads and the uncle. The blow intended for Taads landed flat in his white, ecclesiastical face, but its premature arrival caused the uncle to lose his balance. He briefly continued on his way in a crazy zigzag, hit the cupboard full of *famille rose*, and as the fragments of glass and porcelain were sent flying, slowly slumped to the ground.

"Well done," said Taads. With the help of the monsignor, who had withstood the familial blow amazingly well, they lifted the uncle from the carpet and settled him in an armchair.

It had become empty around the table, at which the three of them resumed their seats. In silence, but with her clown's face glinting with ill-concealed mirth, Petra cleared away the leg of mutton and returned a moment later with a gigantic platter of cheeses and a dark gleaming decanter.

"Mr. Taads," said the priest, "there may be a few things on this mortal earth on which we have the same opinion, but on this at least we can agree: my nephew serves an exemplary glass of port."

They raised their glasses to each other and drank. Inni felt the deep, dark taste pervade his mouth, seductive and mysterious.

"To think," said Terruwe, "that Chamberlain had not even gone to Munich when the grapes of this wine were still hanging in the vineyard in the full heat of the sun."

No one spoke. The priest had closed his eyes and was listening to inaudible voices. When he spoke next, it was in a different voice, as if he were no longer addressing Taads and Inni, but a multitude hidden somewhere behind the grass-colored silk wall hanging.

"Saint Cyprianus teaches me, not you—and this was as early as the second century—that outside the Church there is no salvation. Just as in the days of the Flood there was only one ark in which man could be saved from the death of the body, so there is in the New Covenant only one saving ark, the Catholic Church. And Our Lord himself has said that anyone who refuses to listen to the Church must be regarded as a heathen or a publican. Our Church is holy, for she has a holy founder, a holy doctrine, holy sacraments, and at all times, holy members."

He cut off a piece of Brie and lifted it on the knife to his mouth.

For a moment, Inni saw the creamy, white-yellow substance moving back and forth on his eloquent tongue. Taads, having refilled his glass, raised it against the lamplight with obvious satisfaction and said, in a milder tone than Inni had yet heard him use: "Monsignor, first of all I am grateful to you for receiving that blow on my behalf. You were my other cheek before mine came into question. You have a strong skull and your intellectual capacities have clearly not been impaired, because your thought processes still run along exactly the same doctrinaire track as they always have. But what you don't understand is that I am standing beside the track. I have seen your train going past at least a thousand times. In your perception, which to me would seem blurred by cataract, I am the proverbial erring innocent."

"Not innocent," said the chamberlain. "Not innocent. Only those who *cannot* know the truth are innocent."

"If I err I do so in good faith," said Taads cheerfully. "If faith in God comes through grace, it has not been granted to me."

"God allows the sin of unbelief because he wants us to choose him freely. You can know there is a God through the visible world, through the voice of your conscience, and through divine revelation, and then you may by all means remain a colleague of all that exists—ha-ha-ha—but it is the Church that teaches you what God has revealed, and of that Church you are a member."

"Was."

The priest laughed, but as he was taking a sip of port at the same moment, it turned out badly. He choked and the port squirted out of his mouth and settled in the damask. He coughed the words out. "Was! Was! But we shall never let you go! You have been baptized, you have been counted, you belong to us. When we say that there are so many millions or billions of Catholics in the world, you are one of them. Baptism is a mark for all eternity. You are a member of the body of Christ. Talking about being colleagues! You can never make that undone, no matter what you say!"

"What I find so amazing," said Taads, "is that if someone were to take the trouble to cleave us in two, I mean, to cut each of us vertically in half and then lay the two parts of each on their sides, there would be little visible difference between us."

"A rather painful means of argumentation."

"I said suppose. You have supposed all sorts of things in your life. After all, you get up to some funny casuistical tricks, don't you. Suppose then that our divided brain pans were to be placed on a beautiful tray—this one here, this eighteenth century silver one, is perhaps a bit too good for us. Wouldn't you think it was strange, then, that your gray matter was convinced that one of the three persons residing in your aggregate God was his son, born from a woman who remained a virgin forever but who was nevertheless impregnated by one of the other persons who had 'come upon her' as the Church puts it. And that as a consequence you would two thousand years later walk about in that curious attire of yours, not inelegant but, still, with that funny purple bib, and that your gray matter would send out messages to my gray matter that would be lying so daintily besides yours on the chased silver—just let's go on supposing for a little while longer. And that from this it would have to follow that I am not allowed to think what I think because once upon a time and without my consent—let us be clear—a colleague of yours poured some water on my fontanelle while uttering certain magic formulae, just as in any cannibal club in the jungle."

"Mysterium fidei," said Monsignor Terruwe.

"Mystery my foot," said Taads, rising from the table. "I am going to take my unbaptized dog tor a walk."

The uncle snored. Inni felt himself slowly getting drunk. The priest twirled the crystal port glass between his long, white fingers and sighed.

"Poor soul," he said. His face had taken on a sad expression. He looked at Inni. The mud had definitely darkened in color, sombered by a veil of old-man's sorrow.

"Poor soul. You must not take that in the way people usually use the term. We,"—and he swept his hand through the air as if the entire Catholic church were gathered around him—"we call the souls in purgatory 'poor' souls because they have to suffer greatly and live in separation from God and can do nothing towards shortening their own suffering. Though purgatory . . . purgatory, will he manage to get even there? No one who has been incorporated in the Church, which means all of us here"—and he pointed at the empty chairs—"can be saved unless he perseveres in his love for God, so this applies to Mr. Taads as well. The breach with God is a mortal sin. And the punishment for mortal sin is hell." He closed his eyes. What he saw behind those thin, closed screens must have been terrible, for when he opened them again, it looked as if the mud had darkened a degree further.

"Do you believe in hell?"

"No," said Inni.

"Hell," said Monsignor Terruwe, "is a mystery, and now I am going to have a snooze."

And then there were only two, thought Inni, when the purple-black figure headed as if on invisible rails toward the door. The uncle snored, but on his face there was an expression of reluctance. Someone else, also sitting in that chair, refused to sleep and yet was forced to do so.

Inni had not heard Petra coming in and gave a start when she stroked his hair.

"Oh dearie me, what a pale little boy have we here," she said, and something in the way she spoke caused tears to spring to his eyes. He was not used to people being nice to him.

"Oh my, oh my," she said, "oh my, oh my, oh my. Come on, let's first pack this one off to his room."

She briefly pressed him against herself. He felt her breasts against his chest and clung to her as if he were in danger of drowning.

"What a skinny little feller you are," she said. "Let's dry those little tears of yours, shall we?"

The uncle would not wake from his stupor, but the other one, the unwilling sleeper inside him, stood up and allowed himself to be dragged from the room, up the stairs, and into a bedroom where his aunt was lying in state, like a corpse whose eyes no one had taken the trouble to close.

"Pills," said Petra softly.

They undressed the uncle and lowered him onto the pink catafalque, alongside the other corpse.

"I am ill," said Inni.

Holding his hand, she took him to his room, opened the windows wide, put him down on the bed, and left. Downstairs he heard a clock strike, a strange, high sound marking some impossible hour. The next day, Taads would explain to him that it was a ship's bell striking, but now it seemed as if everything was rattling and clattering, for in this impossible but clearly indicated hour the room rolled from side to side like a ship. He himself was lying in the center of the movement, a still object, until the great rotation lifted him up and drove him as if by a piston to the window. He felt as if he were vomiting out his whole inside and as if even that were not enough, even the empty feeling that followed wanted to get out and kept obstinately and frantically rising and tugging at his gorge. Tears poured out of his eyes. Below him he saw the dark hole of the garden, and although the rolling had now abated, he held on to the windowsill in a desperate grip. His whole life had to come out. Secret substances that for years had lodged resentfully in his feet, his legs, his brains, screamed to be let out. The whole huge crowd of memories and humiliations, his stupid loneliness—everything had to be tipped out into that dark hole of a garden, disappear, become invisible. It had to be thrown out like so much sour, malevolent matter. It had to be cast outside where it would dissolve forever and so would he. He did not want to exist any longer. For the first time in his life this thought became a possibility, simply by being thought.

He heard the door open behind him and knew it was she. Bare feet, he thought, she is in her bare feet. The feet, harbingers of bliss, brought her close behind him. It must be something very thin she was wearing. She crossed her arms over his chest and rocked him gently back and forth as if she knew what he had just been thinking. Without shoes she was scarcely taller than he. A few more times his body convulsed. Then she said softly, "Ssh, ssh."

Not until some time later did she lead him to the washstand, make him dry his tears, blow his nose, clean his teeth, drink. Then she undressed him, put him to bed, turned the light off, and lay down beside him.

The night that had seemed so dark while the lamp was on, now appeared to grow lighter and lighter and began to drive the darkness out of the room. Light or dark, neither could win the battle, and it ended in a still, gray twilight from which they began to loom up to each other. They caressed and kissed, and he saw her slowly changing, too. It was as if her face disappeared and another came in its place, wilder and at the same time remoter. The person that held him and was held by him was very close to him and yet at the same time somewhere else. For the first time he saw that he could bring this about. He found her with his hand, and suddenly she was crouched on her hands and knees, grunting and sighing. Detached she was, far away. It was ominous. A force was breaking loose in her, enabling her to do all the things he would never be able to do—forget her name, this house, this room, and him. And yet it was him she grabbed by the loins, made roll over on top of her, and pulled inside her. Melancholy, desolation, lust, they toiled together in the big bed, sweating and groaning as if in a fight, and all the time it was as if she were in terrible pain, as if she wanted to be released from her body—she, too—as if she wanted at the same time to cling to him and shake him off.

When it was all over, she lay very still, staring at the ceiling with wide-open eyes. He kept looking at her and saw the shadows of her ordinary face slowly resuming their usual places, chasing away the other, more mysterious face that now faded and fled into the vanishing night, among the first sounds of the birds, where it belonged.

"Ah you," she said, slowly sitting up. And all of a sudden changes were taking place inside her as well. Doors were slamming, names returning. Mockery radiated out of her eyes again, and she laughed and said, "There, that makes two mortal sins in one day."

And later, when they were both sitting with their backs leaning against the wall, smoking cigarettes (Golden Fiction, her brand), she put her hands between his legs and laughed. "That big feller of yours has gone small again." And then, with surprise: "But you've got no nozzle. Why is that?"

"I have been circumcised," he said.

"Just like Our Lord?"

"That's right."

She shrieked with laughter.

"When you were a baby?"

"No. Last year."

Time for deep silence.

"Why?"

"Because it hurt when I went to bed with anyone. It was too narrow down there."

"Ooooh." She bent over and looked. He stroked her hair.

"But you're not a Jew, are you?"

"No. That has nothing to do with it."

She sat up straight and pondered about something. Finally she said it.

"You've got sad eyes and devil's eyes. Jewish eyes."

* * *

His circumcision. A friend who lived in the same lodging house had taken him to the surgeon, who was to perform the operation at his home. It was a bright winter afternoon. He was a small Jewish doctor with, most appropriately, a thick German accent and a very Germanic nurse inside whom, thought Inni, the surgeon could easily be tucked away for the night.

The little man told him to undress, peered at him, and said, "A mere trifle. Sister, can ve haf zee injection, ja?"

Suddenly he was lying on a table, and everyone knows that from that position the world looks different. The giantess, who suddenly had no legs and was sailing beside him as if she were sitting in a boat, said, "You will only have a local anesthetic."

Local! He wanted to lift his head to see what was going to happen.

"Lie down still."

Bare winter branches with hoar frost. White, shiny, knobby bones in front of the window. And on the wall Rembrandt's *Anatomy Lesson*—but his patient was already dead. So were Professor Tulp and his painter. Not this Tulp, though. He was standing in a corner, busy with something big and curved that looked like scissors.

"I vas a frient of your poet Schlauerhof." He did not pronounce the second *f* of Slauerhoff. Hofe. "A very remarkable man, but unhappy, very unhappy. Alvayss trouble vith vomen, alvayss arguments. And sick, very sick."

The needle with which the nurse suddenly came sailing along out of the void was big enough to knock out a calf.

"Ho, ho, we'd like to crawl away, would we?" said the nurse good-humoredly and grabbed his fleeing organ. Shot on the wing, he had time to think, but then he saw the needle take a plunge, and he felt the flaming pain of the jab going through the puny victim that lay in her large German hand like a dead mouse.

"Poor Schlauerhof. So many years dead already."

Then they left him lying for a time. The ballet dancer in the reproduction danced on one leg through his tears. Now I can never fuck again, he thought. Never again.

A thin, hairy wrist lifted a gold watch to a pair of dark, gleaming eyes.

"So."

Now there came scissors, a bandage, and a bowl. He could not see properly until the mouse was lifted by the scruff with thumb and forefinger and stared at him from the horizon. The points of the scissors were semicurved, a crooked nickel bird's beak resolutely pecking at his skin. He felt the snips as if something that resisted were being nibbled at. He felt no pain, but there was something else, something he could never explain, not even later. He just felt the sound of the snipping, at the same time soft and crunchy. The smaller hand raised up a bloody rag of skin in the air.

"A mere trifle. As I said. Sew it up, nurse."

Needle and thread—someone was about to darn a sock—sewed him up, sewed up the mouse for good. A mouse sausage. Never again!

He no longer looked. Somewhere in the numb flesh threads were being pulled in and out, in and out. Until there came a movement that had something definitive about it, then nothing more.

"Nurse!" Irritation. "Nurse! A hundred times I have told you to tie ze knot like zeess, not like zat. It is ugly."

"Shall I do it again, doctor?"

"No, don't bozzer. It vas no Praxiteles anyway."

Then there was a lot of messing about down there, but he had said good-bye to it and was living in a small universe of grief. Something had been taken away from him. He heard isolated words, "bismuth . . . plaster . . . plenty, plenty," but he did not want to have anything to do with it anymore. He felt only this strange sadness. Sadness and humiliation.

"Zere. Stand up."

Slowly he let himself slide down from the table.

"Careful!"

Suddenly everybody was walking again. The room had regained its lower half, in which he, too, was standing up, between his legs a proboscis of gauze held together by plaster sticking plaster, in which there burned yellow patches ("bismuth").

"You don't have any nerves, at least."

That's what you think, you sod, you butcher. But I would have bitten off my tongue rather than give a squeal in front of you and that Kriemhilde.

Wide-legged, he staggered about the room, a drunken old man. His whole body had become a mere enclosure around this one defect.

"Ze Arabs never make so much fuss."

They had hoisted him into his trousers, and he had grown dizzy with pain in the process.

In his friend's room, a dark den full of snakes and toads in terrariums, he had waited, with an ever grubbier, ever more sordid penis sheath until he had healed. And now she was looking at it, as seriously as she had listened to his story.

"I think it looks nice," she said.

Slowly she bent over and took him in her mouth. He felt her breasts each time they touched the inside of his calves. Each time her head came up, he saw part of her forehead, the slant of her obliquely set eyebrows. She had closed her eyes, she was working, and there was something devout and pure about it. He was sitting very still, but grimly clutched the sheet with both hands as if the moment, when it came, might blow him away. When it did come, he felt himself draining away, but she remained half thrown forward, her full, beautiful shoulders resting on his knees. Only after some while did she raise herself, her mouth closed. The slanting green eyes laughed, and again, as earlier in the afternoon, she briefly stuck out her tongue with that white, shiny, drifting cloudlet on it, swallowed, and said mockingly, "Three?"

They sat still for a while. He put his hands under her, soft, wet, and delicious. They rocked, shifted, and swayed, muttering soft words, kissing, and whispering spells until the white daylight stood in the room and she laid him down, stroked him, and left. A great addiction had begun. Her fiancé would return from Korea, and Inni would never kiss her or touch her again. They would vanish from each other's lives and die separately. The great black void would eat them and absorb them in separate places, but they would never (never?) forget each other, and his whole life would revolve around women. He would seek this again and again among passersby, friends, whores, and strangers. Women were the rulers of the world, simply because they held him under their command. He would never feel again that he "took" or "conquered" one of them, or whatever other stupid terminology had been invented to conceal the truth: that man, that he, delivered himself up to women with an absolute surrender which invariably caused misunderstanding. If the world was a mystery, then women were the force that maintained this pulsating mystery. They, and only they, had access to it. If anything in this world could be understood, it would have to be understood by means of women. Friendship with men could go a long way, but it only touched the rational side of things, which some women possessed in addition, as an extra. Women were more honest, more direct, than words. They were media. He often had the feeling that women allowed him as far as possible to be a woman, and that without this he would be unable to survive. Not that he had ever wanted to be a woman physically, but in this way, with the woman in his male body, he experienced a mysterious sensation of duplicity. He was what people called a woman's man, but in the sense that in mythology someone can be a birdman. He hated the attitude of most men toward women, for although he did the same things as they, his motivation was different. He *knew* what he sought. Sex was never really what mattered most, sex was merely the delicious vehicle. Women, all women, were a means to come close to, to come within the orbit of, the secret of which they and not the men were the guardians. Through men, but this he would not be able to formulate until much later, you learn how the world is. Through women you learn *what* it is. And this night, on which a thousand other nights, rooms, and bodies would be superimposed, was the most unforgettable of all.

He woke up from a tap on the door and her voice.

"Your aunt wants to know if you're coming to mass."

He was still aware of her smell. Footsteps sounded in the corridors, and downstairs in the hall a small procession was waiting—the uncle, his aunt, and the chamberlain, with the morning sun gleaming on the purple watered silk of his sash.

In church he let Pergolesi, the Gregorian chants, the three slow-dancing dervishes in green, the sermon ("*That* is the mystery which we cannot comprehend: He is both man *and* God. Through his mysterious humanity we share in the divine. Truly we ought to be in ecstasy every day, always, every hour, but we are too small, too wretched . . ."), the consecration, the bells, the candles, flow over him. He peered at the stained-glass windows with their ever-different, ever-same images from a world he had left behind for good. Would she be in church?

To the wooden back of the pew in front of him, brass plates had been fixed with his name coupled to that of his uncle—Donders-Wintrop—but of course she was not allowed to sit there. He saw her only when she came forward to take communion, all the way from the back of the church. Her fourth mortal sin, he thought, and followed her. When she turned from the Communion rail, he caught a brief glimpse of the host on her tongue. Her eyes looked into his, the mockery in them now very lightly veiled by something else, but he would never know what. He loved her, she would confess everything, or not, and after a few weeks she would marry her soldier from Korea. He would never see her again. Now he himself knelt, saw the priest's hand approaching (calf's flesh), momentarily felt an urge to bite into it hard, but instead stuck out his tongue. The dry, light substance fleetingly clung to the soft, moist flesh of his tongue. Then he swallowed and God began to seek His way down to his intestines where—this now seemed inevitable—He would be transformed into seed. And not into anything else.

Taads was waiting by the house. He had already finished his breakfast and had "had some sandwiches packed" for Inni to eat in the car. As they took their leave, his aunt told him she had arranged something with Taads, he would hear about it later. She said she had been pleased to see he had gone to Communion, and then she looked away. Petra he saw once more, but when he approached her, she took a step back and shook her head almost imperceptibly.

"Bye-bye," she said, and turned around and walked off to the kitchen. He retained the vision of her green eyes.

His aunt had settled a sum of money on him of which he could draw the interest. It was not much, said Taads, but enough for someone of his age to manage on. Nor did he have to worry about the future, but about that no details were provided at this stage.

In the years that followed, he saw Arnold Taads regularly, always according to the same ritual: walk, reading hour, goulash, always in the same bitter atmosphere of self-inflicted, deadly loneliness aggravated by growing maniacal insomnia. His contempt for mankind turned to savage hate. The winters spent in his "deserted valley" became longer. In 1960 Inni received a first and last letter from him.

"Dear friend, my dog Athos has died. He had a brain tumor. I shot him myself, which I am certain he did not realize. The shot echoed unbearably long—it is very empty here in the mountains. I buried him under the snow. Best wishes, regards to Zita. Yours, Arnold Taads."

A few months later he heard from his aunt that Arnold Taads was dead. As he had not turned up in the village on his usual shopping expedition, a rescue team had gone out to look for him. They had found him, frozen to death, his rucksack empty, not very far from his hut. Inni wondered whether he had sounded the Alpine distress signal. But no one would ever know. The frozen man was cremated, and now there existed no longer in the world an Arnold Taads.

III PHILIP TAADS 1973

The Philosophy of Tea . . . is a moral geometry, inasmuch as it defines our sense of proportion to the universe.

Okakura Kakuzo
The Book of Tea

Ne pas naître est sans contredit la meilleure formule qui soit. Elle n'est malheureusement à la portée de personne.

E. M. Cioran
De l'inconvénience d'être né

There were days, thought Inni Wintrop, when it seemed as if a recurrent, fairly absurd phenomenon were trying to prove that the world is an absurdity that can best be approached with nonchalance, because life would otherwise become unbearable.

There were days, for instance, when you kept meeting cripples, days with too many blind people, days when you saw three times in succession a left shoe lying by the roadside. It seemed as if all these things were trying to mean something, but could not. They left only a vague sense of unease, as if somewhere there existed a dark plan for the world that allowed itself to be hinted at only in this clumsy way.

The day on which he was destined to meet Philip Taads, of whose existence he had hitherto been unaware, was the day of the three doves. The dead one, the live one, and the dazed one, which could not possibly have been one and the same, because he had seen the dead one first. These three, he thought later, had made an attempt at annunciation that had succeeded insofar as it had made the encounter with Taads the Younger more mysterious.

It was now 1973, and Inni had turned forty in a decade he did not approve of. One ought not, he felt, to live in the second half of any century, and this particular century was altogether bad. There was something sad and at the same time ridiculous about all these fading years piling on top of one another until at last the millennium arrived. And they contained a contradiction, too: in order to reach the hundred, and in this case the thousand, that had to be completed, one had to add them up; but the feeling that went with the process seemed to have more to do with subtraction. It was as if no one, especially not Time, could wait for those ever dustier, ever higher figures finally to be declared void by a revolution of a row of glittering, perfectly shaped noughts, whereupon they would be relegated to the scrap heap of history. The only people apparently still sure of anything in these days of superstitious expectation were the Pope, the sixth of his name already, a white-robed Italian with an unusually tormented face that faintly resembled Eichmann's, and a number of terrorists of different persuasions, who tried in vain to anticipate the great witches' cauldron. The fact that he was now forty no longer in itself bothered Inni very much.

"Forty," he said, "is the age at which you have to do everything for the third time, or else you'll have to start training to be a cross-tempered old man," and he had decided to do the latter.

After Zita, he had had a long-lasting affair with an actress who had finally, in self-preservation, turned him out of the house like an old chair.

"What I miss most about her," he said to his friend the writer, "is her absence. These people are never at home. You get addicted to that."

He now lived alone and intended to keep it that way. The years passed, but even this was noticeable only in photographs. He bought and sold things, was not addicted to drugs, smoked less than one packet of Egyptian cigarettes a day, and drank neither more nor less than most of his friends.

This was the situation on the radiant June morning when, on the bridge between the Heerenstraat and the Prinsenstraat, a dove flew straight at him as if to bore itself into his heart. Instead, it smashed against a car approaching from the Prinsengracht. The car drove on and the dove was left lying in the street, a gray and dusty, suddenly silly-looking little thing. A blonde-haired girl got off her bicycle and went up to the dove at the same time as Inni.

"Is it dead, do you think?" she asked.

He crouched down and turned the bird onto its back. The head did not turn with the rest of the body and continued to stare at the road surface.

"Finito," said Inni.

The girl put her bike away.

"I daren't pick it up," she said, "Will you?"

She used the familiar form of you. As long as they still do that, I am not yet old, thought Inni, picking up the dove. He did not like doves. They were not a bit like the image he used to have of the Holy Ghost, and the fact that all those promises of peace had never come to anything was probably their fault as well. Two white, softly cooing doves in the garden of a Tuscan villa, that was all right, but the gray hordes marching across the Dam Square with spurs on their boots (their heads making those idiotic mechanical pecking movements) could surely have nothing to do with a Spirit which had allegedly chosen that particular shape in which to descend upon Mary.

"What are you going to do with it?" asked the girl.

Inni looked around and saw on the bridge a wooden skip belonging to the Council. He went up to it. It was full of sand. Gently he laid the dove in it. The girl had followed him. An erotic moment. Man with dead dove, girl with bike and blue eyes. She was beautiful.

"Don't put it in there," she said. "The workmen will chuck it straight into the canal."

What does it matter whether it rots away in sand or in water, thought Inni, who often claimed he would prefer to be blown up after his death. But this was not the moment to hold a discourse on transience.

"Are you in a hurry?" he asked.

"No."

"Give me that bag then." From her handlebar hung a plastic bag, one from the Athenaeum Book Store.

"What's in there?"

"A book by Jan Wolkers."

"It can go in there then," said Inni. "There's no blood."

He put the dove in the bag.

"Jump on the back."

He took her bike without looking at her and rode off.

"Hey," she said. He heard her rapid footsteps and felt her jumping on the back of the bike. In the shop windows he caught brief glimpses of something that looked like happiness. Middle-aged gentleman on girl's bicycle, girl in jeans and white sneakers on the back.

He rode down the Prinsengracht to the Haarlemmerdijk and from a distance saw the barriers of the bridge going down. They got off, and as the bridge slowly rose, they saw the second dove. It was sitting inside one of the open metal supports under the bridge, totally unconcerned as it allowed itself to be lifted up like a child on the Ferris wheel.

For a moment Inni felt an impulse to take the dead dove out of the plastic bag and lift it up like a peace offering to its slowly ascending living colleague, but he did not think the girl would like it. And besides, what would be the meaning of such a gesture? He shuddered, as usual not knowing why. The dove came down again and vanished invulnerably under the asphalt. They cycled on, to the Westerpark. With her small, brown hands, the girl dug a grave in the damp, black earth, somewhere in a corner.

"Deep enough?"

"For a dove, yes."

He laid the bird, which was now wearing its head like a hood on its back, into the hole. Together they smoothed the loose earth on top of it.

"Shall we go and have a drink?" he asked.

"All right."

Something in this minimal death, either the death itself or the summary ritual surrounding it, had made them allies. Something now had to happen, and if this something had anything to do with death, it would not be obvious. He cycled along the Nassaukade. She was not heavy. This was what pleased him most about his strange life—that when he had gotten up that morning, he had not known that he would now be cycling here with a girl at his back, but that such a possibility was always there. It gave him, he thought, something invincible. He looked at the faces of the men in the oncoming cars, and he knew that his life, in its absurdity, was right. Emptiness, loneliness, anxiety—these were the drawbacks—but there were also compensations, and this was one of them. She was humming softly and then fell silent. She said suddenly, as if she had taken a decision, "This is where I live."

It was more like an order than a statement. He obeyed and followed her pointing finger into the Second Hugo de Grootstraat. With a heavy iron chain she tied her bike to a parking meter and opened a door. Without a word she led the way, up endless flights of stairs. Promiscuity in Amsterdam had a lot to do with stairs, especially in younger circles. He climbed calmly behind the sneakers, regulating his breathing so that he would not be panting when they came to the top. They climbed very high indeed, to a small room with a skylight. Plants, books in an orange crate, an Elvis Presley poster, a copy of *Vrij Nederland*, breathtakingly tiny, white and light-blue panties strung out on a line in front of the open window. The notion, he thought, of happiness mingled with melancholy was a cliché, as was this room, as was he himself in this room. It had all happened before. It had to be longed for every time afresh, but it had already happened. She put on a record that he vaguely recognized, and turned towards him. This, he understood, was a generation that did not waste time. They put you on and they took you off like a glove, efficient actions following quick decisions. Sometimes it was more like a form of work than anything else.

She stood facing him. She was almost as tall as he, and he looked straight into her blue eyes. They stood solemnly, but with a gravity you could see the bottom of, a gravity without structure. She had not suffered yet, and that was not accidental either. Suffering, he had learned, could be refused, as it commonly was these days.

She undressed him, he undressed her, and they lay down side by side. She smelled of girl. He stroked her, and twice she pushed his hand a fraction, saying "No, not here, there," and then appeared to forget him. The body as gadget. She came without a hitch in the mechanism. There was something very *sweet* about it, he thought. His own performance seemed like a huge car in a narrow English country lane. A few years later, half the American car industry would slump, as a result of just such an anachronism. There was still a lot to be learned in beds. He lay still for a while and felt the small (tennis? basketball?) air-cooled hands stroking his back.

"Gee," she said. And then, "How old are you?"

He could see the handwriting in which she would enter it in her diary (no, you oaf, they don't keep diaries these days) and said, "Forty-five." It was the first thing that came into his head.

"I've never been with anyone as old as that."

Records—that was another thing they suffered from. But you could hardly blame them.

"You'd better not make a habit of it."

"I quite liked it."

An immense languor flowed through his body, but he got up. She rolled a cigarette.

"You want one?"

"No thanks."

He washed by the washstand and knew she was not looking at him. He dressed. Summer, it was soon over. Life was a happening.

"Where are you going?"

"I have to meet a friend."

It was true. He had arranged to see Bernard Roozenboom. Bernard was in his fifties. Together they were almost a hundred. Did they still call that friends at her age? He went to the bed, knelt beside her, and caressed her face.

"Shall I see you again sometime?" he asked.

"No. I have a boyfriend."

"I see." He got up. Not too quickly, because of the occasion, and not too slowly, so as not to seem too old. Then he walked out of the room on tiptoe—he did not know why but suspected the worst (my little daughter is asleep).

"Bye."

"Bye."

Not until he was several blocks away did it occur to him that neither of them had asked the other's name. He stopped and looked at a window display of electrical goods. Irons and orange squeezers stared back at him. What were names, anyway? What difference would it have made to this episode if he had known her name? None, and yet he felt there was something wrong with an age in which you could go namelessly to bed with someone. But then you've never thought otherwise, he said aloud to himself, and returned to his earlier thought: What are names? Arrangements of letters that, when you pronounce them, form a word by which you can somehow address or refer to a person. Usually these shorter or longer arrangements had distant roots in the Bible or in church history and were therefore connected, in ways that had become obscure to almost everyone, with human beings who had really lived once, which made it all the more mysterious. That you did not choose your own name was arbitrary enough, but suppose that on reaching adulthood you could, in the manner of the Anabaptists, choose a name for yourself. To what extent would you then *be* that name? He read the names on the front doors he passed. But they were surnames, which made it even worse. De Jong, Zorgdrager, Rooseveld, Stuut, Lie. Live bodies lived here, bearing those names until they died. After that, their bodies would disintegrate, but the names that had belonged to them would continue to linger for some time in registers, surveys, and computers. And yet, somewhere in the eleven provinces, there must once upon a time have been a field in which roses had grown, and something of that once-existing field had been preserved in the white italic lettering on the door.

There was something disagreeable about these thoughts that did not fit in with the plans he had for today. Today was a happy day, he had decided, and nothing could move him from his resolve. Besides, this first summer morning had thrown a girl into his lap who had driven the winter cold from his bones. He ought to be grateful. He decided to call her Dovey, and stepped inside a phone booth to tell Bernard that he would be a little late.

About an hour later, as he was walking across the hot, noisy Rokin on his way to Bernard's shop, he had a pleasant feeling of anticipation. Bernard Roozenboom was the last of a line of renowned art dealers and had entrenched himself in his shop like a crab, as he put it. The window, in which usually only one object was displayed, an Italian Renaissance drawing or a small painting by a not too well known master of the Dutch school, seemed to aim more at putting visitors off than at attracting them.

"Your place looks so forbidding and closed, I'm sure you have raised the culture barrier by at least a meter," Inni had said to him once.

Bernard had shrugged. "Anyone who wants to see me can find me," he had replied. "All those upstarts, newly rich builders, heart specialists, and dentists"—a tone of intense scorn set in—"buy *modern* art. In *galleries*. To buy my stuff you need intelligence, and not just ordinary intelligence but judgment as well. And this is in short supply these days. There is a lot of lazy money around, and lazy money knows nothing about anything."

Inni had never met any customers there besides foreigners and one famous art historian, but that meant nothing. In a business like Bernard's, one customer could make up for six months, and in any case Bernard was rich. To get to him you had to go through three doors. On the first one, the street door, his name was painted in gold lettering—"English lettering," said Bernard. Having ventured through this door, you were standing in a minuscule hall, unexpectedly quiet, that led to a second door. By then, the Rokin was already far away. The moment you touched the gleamingly polished knob of the second door, graceful chimes would tinkle. You then arrived in the second hall ("Isn't that what you Catholics call limbo, or would it already be purgatory?"), and usually no one appeared. Through the net curtains forming the rear of the display window, some filtered daylight fell across the Persian carpet, which muffled every footstep, and on the two, at most three, paintings on the wall, which somehow conjured up thoughts of money rather than art ("My velvet mousetrap"). After a lapse of some time, a slow shadow would stir in the glow of the lamp behind the window—a glow that at this distance reached no higher than your knees ("I live in the underworld but I am not looking for anyone"). To get there you had to descend some steps ("Three steps, just like the

Gold Coach, but the House of Orange does not buy art"). The room itself was small and dark. There were two desks, one for Bernard and one for a secretary, when there was one. For the rest, the furniture consisted of a heavy armchair, a threadbare two-seater chesterfield, and a couple of bookcases full of leather-bound reference books that Bernard did not need to consult because he knew everything already.

"Hello there," said Bernard. "I can't shake hands with you because I am being manicured. This is Mrs. Theunissen. She has held sway over my nails ever since I was a baby."

"How do you do," said Inni.

The lady nodded. Under a fierce little operating lamp, Bernard's right hand lay like an anesthetized patient in her left hand. Slowly, one by one, she filed his pink nails over a bowl of water. Until the day Inni first set eyes on Kees Verwey's portrait of Lodewijk van Deyssel, he had always thought that Bernard Roozenboom resembled le Baron de Charlus as he imagined him, although le baron would probably not have been pleased to look like what he called "an Israelite." Though what an Israelite was supposed to look like, no one could be sure of these days, ever since photographs of golden-haired female Israeli soldiers had appeared in the papers. The aristocratic cast of Bernard's nose stemmed from his own Renaissance drawings, his scant hair had that Nordic sandy color that goes so well with tweeds, and his pale blue eyes had nothing of the glowing black cherries of the author of *à la Recherche du temps perdu*, or, as Bernard preferred to say, "perdà." Besides, no one except Proust and his readers had ever seen le baron, if it was possible at all to see someone made of words. However, if anyone was really training to be a cross-tempered old man, which was what Charlus and van Deyssel had been after all, each in his own way, it was Bernard. Skepticism, arrogance, aloofness, everything in his face, conspired to make the biting aphorisms he employed against friend and foe all the more wounding; and this tendency of his was further strengthened by financial independence, a razor-sharp intelligence, vast erudition, and obstinate bachelorhood. His clothes, made to measure in London, concealed with some difficulty a heavy, somewhat rustic figure. His whole appearance (as he said himself) smacked defiantly of bygone times.

"Well, my friend, I suppose you've come to show me some more rubbish?" Bernard Roozenboom was the only person who refused to call him by his name, now that he was forty. "*Inni*. It makes me laugh. That isn't a name, it's a little noise. But Inigo is even more ridiculous. Some people think that if they give their child the name of a celebrity, an inherent genius will be supplied at a stroke. Inigo Wintrop, the world-famous architect. Inigo Wintrop's revolutionary designs in the Tate Gallery."

Inni put the two items he had brought on the secretary's desk.

"Let's have a look."

"When you've finished." He did not want to make himself look silly in front of the manicurist.

"I won't deny you have a fairly good nose," Bernard had once said, "but at best you're a dilettante, and frankly you are just a common peddler."

Inni sat down on the chesterfield and started leafing through the *Financial Times*.

"Boeing has slipped, KLM has slipped, and the dollar isn't feeling too well either," said Bernard, who knew a little about Inni's financial affairs. "If you had bought that Roghman drawing from me last year, you wouldn't have to look so glum now. At least you wouldn't have *lost* anything then."

"I didn't know you read this," said Inni, pushing the pink paper away.

"I don't. A customer left it here."

"I suppose he came to buy an Appel."

"I am not a greengrocer," said Bernard Roozenboom. "Show Mrs. Theunissen your nails, then Uncle Bernard will treat you to a nail shine."

"No thanks, I always bite them myself."

"Help yourself to the port then."

Inni felt comfortable. He liked the mahogany cupboard in which the port was kept, and he liked the crystal decanter and the seventeenth-century glass whose deep-green color shone in the glare of Mrs. Theunissen's lamp. The idea of money as such no longer interested him, now that he was getting older. Money that merely remained money, rotted away, lay stinking and moldering somewhere. It was rejuvenated yet at the same time eaten away—growth and disease—processes unpleasantly canceling each other out, a cancer attacking everyone that handled it to a greater or lesser degree. Here in Bernard's domain, money had been blended with a nobler element. This was not the helter-skelter of the scramblers and the grabbers but the still world of objects expressing genius and power, where money lagged a long way behind knowledge, love, collector's mania, and the concomitant sacrifices and blind irrationality. With closed eyes he could picture the room above his friend's office. There, in tall cupboards, lay the countless drawings that formed the core of Bernard's highly specialized collection. Certainly, these drawings also expressed money, but at the same time they stood for something that would endure if for whatever reason they lost their monetary value. And then there was the secret room containing Bernard's private collection, which he hardly ever showed to anyone but which, as Inni knew, although his cynical friend would never say so, embodied the meaning of his life. Sitting here, he felt the silent power of these things around him, things that in a mysterious way forged a link between him and long-vanished people and times.

When the manicurist had gone, Bernard picked up Inni's folder from the desk. In silence he peered at the first page. Inni waited.

"If you were somebody with a bit more of a clue to things, you would know what I am holding in my hand," Bernard said finally.

"It's because I am somebody with a bit of a clue that you *are* holding it in your hand."

"Well done. And yet you don't know what it is."

"At least I knew what it was not."

"What did you pay for it?"

"Too little, I think, considering the fuss you're making. What is it?"

"It isn't all that special, but it's nice."

"Nice?"

"I am crazy about Sibyls."

"Yes, that much I could see for myself, that it was a Sibyl. I *can* read, you know."

"A Catholic schoolboy knows his Latin."

"Exactly. But who is it by?"

"It's a Baldini."

"Is it." Inni had never heard of Baldini, and he wondered how terrible that was.

"Actually, we know hardly anything about Baldini," said Bernard, constructing with this "we" a worldwide congregation of scholars around himself, which naturally excluded Inni.

"Neither do we," said Inni, and waited. Now the cat and mouse game was due to begin. The nice thing about friends was that you knew them, so that they did not easily disappoint you.

"It is really a rather stiff, labored etching," said Bernard. "Clumsy. Our friend Baldini was no great master. But he was early, that he was. Vasari mentions him. Let's say a shadow of the shadow of Botticelli."

Inni had read Vasari, on Bernard's advice, actually, but he could not remember anything about a Baldini.

"Baldini?"

"Baccio Baldini. Died before 1500. Why did you buy this?"

"I thought it was rather curious. And this N here, which has been crossed out so childishly—I thought that was amusing."

"Hm." In the clumsy banderole in the top right hand corner of the etching was a legend the last word of which was REGINA. It had first said RENGINA, but the N had been crossed out later with the sort of cross illiterates use for their signature, earnest and conclusive.

"I see. But why curious?"

They looked at the Libyan Sibyl together. She was seated inside a wide tent of stiffly etched clothing and appeared to be reading. Behind her, her veil billowed in a gust of wind that inexplicably did not seem to disturb anything else in the picture. The upper part of her cloak was so richly decorated that her face floated white and empty above it. The eyes, which seemed to be looking through or across the book that lay open in her lap, gave her face an air of timid, dreamy absentmindedness. An absentmindedness, thought Inni, that had continued for almost five hundred years. He saw the dead dove before him again. A drawing of a dove could live on, but a dove could not. Such a thought signified nothing, and yet it was awesome. A big word. Enigmatic.

"She is hatching some sinister prophecy," said Bernard. "She has got rabbit ears, but that is probably the Libyan in her."

"It looks more like a woodcut," said Inni.

"Niello," replied Bernard, and when Inni did not react, "Niello is working in black enamel. That is where the technique comes from." And then suddenly, "It's not a bad little thing, really."

The pale head bore a crown of flowers out of which flowed a veil that, behind the body, suddenly described a strange curve that defied every law of nature. The wreathed head was crowned once more by a small pyramid-shaped, closed object, pierced on either side by three long thin leaves or feathers.

Partly because her own, no doubt tiny, ivory ears were invisible under the thick, un-Libyan blonde plaited coiffure, these did indeed give the Sibyl the appearance of an elegant female human rabbit.

"Let's get her record out, shall we," said Bernard. "Come upstairs with me. I am the beacon to light the path of the ignorant that wander in darkness." Corridors, and a great deal of fumbling with keys. Inni suddenly had to think of the girl again.

Bernard took a book out of a case and put it down in front of Inni. *Early Italian Engravings from the National Gallery of Art*. In alphabetical order.

Inni leafed through it and found his Sibyl. It gave him a feeling of pride, as if the etching had only just now begun to exist. He looked at his find with a little more respect.

"So it hangs in Washington," he said.

"Whether it hangs there I don't know. They've got plenty of other things to hang. But it's there all right. You'd better read all about it. But no, that's too much; it's a very thorough book. I'll have a photocopy made, and you can take that along with you when you go to Sotheby's."

"When *you* go to Sotheby's," said Inni.

"All right then. If I am going there anyway."

Bernard fetched another book. "Note this, my friend," he said. "Several solid kilograms of *love*, because this masterpiece was made with the ingredients of the exceptional: endless patience, vast knowledge, but most of all love. It's written by Frits Lugt, a very rich old man who turned his money into time, the quintessence of alchemy. Look. All the collectors' marks. Isn't that delightful. I don't suppose our little art dealer had noticed that, had he?"

"Noticed what?"

"That there was a collector's mark on your etching. What else do you imagine this is?" He pointed at a strange, small, graceful mark on the back of the etching.

"I wonder if we can find that anywhere."

Inni read the title of the book: "*Les marques de collections de dessins et d'estampes*, Frits Lugt, Amsterdam 1921."

"Help me look for it," said Bernard.

Inni examined the mark. Two curious insect legs without a body, flanking three vertical lines that ended in a tiny circle.

"It looks rather like the sexual symbol of a Red Indian tribe."

"Go on," said Bernard. "The eye of the beholder. Red Indians never cared much for early Renaissance. If you try hard enough we'll find it in no time."

"Maybe it isn't in there."

"There speaks the contemptible generation. Everything is in Lugt."

He was right. Two insect legs were stylized *R*'s set back to back, the initials of Freiherr C. Rolas du Rosey (1862), 'général prussien, Dresde. "*Estampes et dessins*, that tallies," said Bernard. "Those were the days." He read half aloud, ". . . importante collection d'objets d'art, de curiosités . . . lui-même a dressé première catalogue raisonné . . . well, well, those German Junkers! . . . première vente 8 avril 1863 . . . many engravings . . . not very remarkable . . . ha, ha . . . auctioned in Leipzig . . . prices not very high . . . and so by the mysterious roundabout way of all things, arrived in Rome, cloaca mundi . . . where the great connoisseur Wintrop . . . immediately recognizes an etching by Baldini . . . at an auction . . . in a little shop . . ."

"A little shop."

" . . . and buys it for a song. Congratulations. You're bound to make something out of it. So you won't need to eat into your capital for a few months. "It'll give you the feeling you've done some work, too. And that other thing, what is that?"

"A Japanese print."

"My God."

"You can have a look at it, can't you?"

"No. Take it to Riezenkamp. He's the expert. I know nothing

about them. I can't *see* anything in those prints. As far as I am concerned, they come from Mars. All those stereotyped curved little noses, those ghastly doll's faces, with too little or too much expression or none at all. Just up your street. Omnivore, omnifume, omniboit, omnivoit. You are incapable of selecting—a sure sign of lack of class. That's why you're nothing more than a dabbler. That is somebody who likes everything. Life's too short. The human condition does not allow it. You can only really find a thing beautiful if you know something about it. He who does not select will perish in the morass. Carelessness, lack of attention, not really knowing anything about anything, the muddy face of dilettantism. The second half of the twentieth century. More opportunities for everyone. More people knowing less about more. The spread of knowledge over as large an area as possible. He who wants to skate over the surface will fall through the ice. Thus spake Bernard Roozenboom."

They went down the stairs.

"You know where to find Riezenkamp?"

"Spiegelgracht."

"Give him my regards. He is an honorable man."

Outside, Inni tumbled into the sunlight again. Everything and everyone seemed to have been dipped in a layer of happiness. The city that in recent years had acquired the appearance of a fortress under demolition, seemed aglow. Light danced in the water of the Rokin Canal. He turned into the Spui and saw in the distance the light-green shimmer of the trees in front of the Béguinage. There the third dove appeared to him, and it did something he had never yet seen a dove do: it created a work of art, for which, as is fitting, it was prepared to make a great sacrifice. With tremendous force it flew straight at Bender's store window, behind which the grand pianos and harpsichords stood waiting motionlessly for future geniuses. It caused a loud bang. For a moment it looked as if the bird was stuck to the glass for good. But, to avoid crashing to the ground, it fluttered desperately in place and then flew off like an airplane out of control. What remained was a work of art, for just above head level on the windowpane, there appeared in street dirt and dust the perfect shape of a dove in flight, feather by feather, with outspread wings. The crash had imprinted the dove's incorporeal double on the glass.

What was it these doves were trying to tell him? He did not know, but decided that this latest sibyllic communication, prophecy, warning, could be no truly sinister portent. After all, unlike its dead colleague, this dove had, however unsteadily, flown away into the azure sky, leaving behind only its spirit, albeit in the form of dust.

At Riezenkamp's there reigned a different kind of dignity from that at Bernard's. A stock-still bronze buddha, his right hand stretched out in a gesture seemingly expressing rebuff, which, as Inni learned later, was precisely not the case, stared across the Spiegelgracht into a total and everlasting nothingness. A faint smile played about his sensuous lips, but otherwise the expression was severe. The pyramid-shaped headdress he wore reminded Inni fleetingly of the Libyan Sibyl. Doves, oracles, preachers—it was obvious that higher powers were aiming at him today. He stared at the disproportionately long, black earlobe of the squat bronze statue. Someone who had been alive in the sixth century and whose image was now sitting comfortably in a shop window in a world that had not even existed during his lifetime.

Suddenly Inni felt his attention being drawn toward something else, so strongly that a natural law seemed to be at work, forcing his poor body to turn away from the Enlightened One and walk with leaden feet to the next window. There a small man of oriental appearance was staring into the showcase, oblivious of the world. Both the man and the object he was looking at were destined to play a role in his life. Since the one would never be thinkable without the other, he assumed that the bowl—for it was a bowl they were both looking at now—had at this significant moment drawn him, through the man, toward itself. It stood all on its own in the showcase, the floor of which was covered by silk of an indefinable shade of green. The small stand on which it stood was also green, as were the background and the side walls. A black bowl. But with that nothing had yet been said.

Some things expressed tranquillity; others manifested power. But it was not always clear what this power was based on. Beauty, perhaps, but this word had an ethereal connotation that seemed to contradict power. Perfection, but this evoked, wrongly perhaps, an idea of symmetry and logic that was decisively absent here. It was a bowl, so of course it was round, but you could certainly not say that it was perfectly round. Its height was not the same everywhere. The walls—no, that was not the right way to put it—the inside and the outside gleamed and yet had a certain roughness. If it had stood in a different place or among several other objects, you might have taken it for the work of a not untalented Danish potter. But in this solitary position of strength, that was out of the question. There it was, on its little stand, black, faintly lustrous yet rough, on a foot that seemed too slender for its *poids*, which of course meant weight, though if you had said *weight*, you would not have expressed it precisely. It stood there and existed. Semantics, this, but how else could you say it? That it lived? That, too, was a weak bid. Perhaps the best way to put it would be that this pot, bowl, or whatever you cared to call the solitary object, looked as if it had come into being spontaneously instead of having been made by man. It was literally *sui generis*. It had created itself and ruled over itself and over anyone who looked at it. One could quite easily be afraid of this bowl.

Inni had a feeling as if the man beside him wanted to say something to him. This, or else the idea that he might be disturbing the man in his trance, made him go inside. A short staircase led up to the shop. Here he was in Asia, or rather, in a rarefied, lofty abstraction of Asia. The tall man in chalk-stripe suit who came up to him formed a contrast with the place, but in such a way as to lend to the sparse but cleverly arranged objects an air of banal realism that made it seem plausible that they might actually be sold. For the first time it struck Inni how very strange was the job of an art dealer.

"Mr. Wintrop," said the man, "I have heard about you already. Bernard Roozenboom phoned me just now."

And had no doubt given him a perfect description, thought Inni. How would he have described him? He would have to ask him. So like Bernard, to phone. Inni would never know whether this was in order to help him or in order to claim part of the credit in the event that he really had hit on something special.

"I gather you make splendid discoveries from time to time."

"I have been lucky once or twice," said Inni, "but in your field I am blind and deaf. You may laugh at me if you like."

Inni unwrapped the print and handed it to the man, who looked at it in silence for a moment and then put it down.

"I am certainly not going to laugh at you. You have come very close to greatness here. This print, this woodcut, can be regarded as belonging to the ukiyoe period. I don't know whether the term means anything to you. Transient life, a concept in Japanese art history. If you like, I will explain it to you some day. But the man who made this is certainly not one of the great ones, like, for instance, an Utamaro. If he had been, and you had bought it, let us say, by accident and therefore for very little money—but frankly, that would have been quite impossible, although you never know—you would have been able to live in luxury on Capri for a long, long time."

Capri of all places! But never mind.

"What is it then?"

Riezenkamp's large, white face hung briefly over the print as if he wanted to nibble the female figure off the paper. His eyes went from right to left, from top to bottom.

"It's a pleasant little thing but rather crude. I hope you didn't pay much for it?"

"Not a lot."

"Good. Look, I'll show you the difference." He went away and returned with a large book.

How many books have I seen today? thought Inni.

"This is a famous print by Utamaro. Even if you aren't trained in looking at these things, you ought to feel something."

It was a portrait of a woman. Riezenkamp's hand made a few sketching movements and then came to rest on the margin of the page.

"When you look at it consciously for the first time, you won't find many points of contact. With the things you're accustomed to looking at, I mean."

He was right. In the large, light-colored area of her face, there were no shadows, no nuances. Sensuous it most certainly was, but far away, unapproachable. The tiny mouth stood slightly open, the eyes without lashes were also very small and seemed to express nothing, and the nose was a single curved line. Without any change in color the area of the face ran down into the décolleté, which with the most minimal of lines suggested the swell of the right breast, strangely in the lower left-hand corner of the print. The way in which the green kimono bulged forward and up at the left shoulder did not seem logical to Inni, but neither had that peculiar backward billow of the Sibyl's veil been logical, except that there it had looked clumsy and here it possessed an indefinable dramatic force.

"What do those characters mean in the top left-hand corner?"

"That is the courtesan's name, and the name of her brothel."

He looked again. The only lewd thing about the print was that minimal breast line. The face remained abstract. There was no reason to touch her. Perhaps that was forbidden anyway. You weren't supposed to kiss Amsterdam whores either. But geishas weren't whores.

"And down here?"

"The editor's seal and the name of the artist."

"If," said the voice which was now above him and had a curious upper-class quality—a sound that screened off a territory and therefore also seemed quite remote from everything oriental—"if you were to regard the colors merely as colors, you would notice how sophisticated the composition is. Look at this piled-up shiny black mass of hair, for instance. It all looks so simple, but of course it isn't. Your print . . ." the voice hesitated, "your print is very nice. It was an everyday product in those days, and it probably comes from some booklet or other, a guide to the red-light district shall we say, ha-ha. Actually, it's much more recent than this one, but to us it simply has the attraction of the exotic. Would you like a drink?"

"Thank you."

Inni rose from his stooping posture and looked straight into the eyes of the man who was still standing outside the display window.

"An attentive observer," he said.

"Very," said Riezenkamp. "And not only that. He knows all about it as well. With such a man as a customer I could live. But the true fanatics don't have any money. It may sound strange coming from me, but since art has become more and more a question of investment, it isn't so much fun any longer. The wrong people buy the good stuff. Or rather, they have it bought for them. By highly skilled servants who have first sold themselves."

He waved, and the man outside nodded. "He'll be coming in presently. An odd fish if you don't know him, but I like him. And one day he'll buy something from me, something great. Not that it matters . . ." The voice trailed away because at that instant two Japanese entered, together with the attentive stranger. Only now did Inni notice how very oriental the man looked. He distinguished himself from the Japanese in their smart suits and ties only by his clothes. White linen trousers, a white collarless shirt, bare feet in the simplest of sandals. The Japanese remained standing in the doorway and made a series of small bows. Riezenkamp's tall figure bowed in return, and he disappeared into his office with them. Without a sound, the man in white crossed the room and paused by a screen. Then he said suddenly, "I saw you were interested in the raku bowl."

Inni turned toward him and said, "Only in the object as such. I know nothing about these things, and I have never seen anything like it before. It is as if it emits some kind of threat."

"Threat?"

"Yes, nonsense of course. I heard myself say it but it wasn't what I meant. I really wanted to say power."

"If that is what you wanted to say, you would have said it. You meant exactly what you said, of course. Threat."

Together they walked in the direction of the window. The bowl was now below them, so that he could look into it, and it was as if he were looking into the depth of an eye, or into a deep black pool, infinitely scaled down. The bowl stared back, hollow, black-gleaming, the envoy of a universe in which the uninitiated had no business.

"Kuroraku," said the man beside him. It sounded like a magic formula, as if by uttering these words, one could curb the bowl's mysterious power.

Half an hour later, Inni knew more about raku pottery than he ever could, or would want to, remember, for as the soft, somewhat drawling voice encapsulated him in names of masters and bowls, thrusting dynasties of potters upon him as if they were the kings of lost mythical realms—Raku IX . . . Raku X—he knew at the same time that this art, not only the bowls but also the kakemonos, the buddha statues, the netsukes, would always remain alien to him, because it stemmed from a culture and a tradition that were not his and could never become his. For the first time he had the feeling that he was too old for something. All this might be part of the world in which he lived, but each of these objects had a meaning for transcending its external beauty. As long as he only looked at it and could regard this looking as a purely aesthetic experience, it was all right, but he was repulsed by the realization that there was so much to be learned about each separate object. He would need another life for it, he would have to be born again, because his one and only birth had excluded him from this strange world by virtue of the moment and the place at which it had occurred. Beyond his will, a choice had been made, and he had to stick to it.

Bernard was right. There were things one had to renounce, even if they were possible. Now that he had reached the age of forty, he would never become a pianist or learn Japanese, he was sure of it. And at the same time this certainty made him feel sad, as if life was at last beginning to make its limitations clear, and death was in sight. It was not true that all things were possible. Perhaps all things had been possible, but they were no longer. You were what you had, perhaps unintentionally, chosen to be, and he was a person who could read a Romanesque tympanum, who knew what symbols belonged to each of the Evangelists, who was able to recognize the allusions to Greek mythology in a Renaissance painting, and who knew which attribute went with each saint in Christian iconography. "Und," he sang inaudibly while the didactic voice beside him continued, "das ist meine Welt, und sonst gar nichts."

Once, in the Cathedral of Toledo, he had seen a group of Japanese tourists, guidebooks in hand, walking past the stations of the cross. At each station they crowded around their leader like a small herd. All that was missing was a sheep dog to bite them in the ankle if they lagged behind. But they did not lag behind; they listened attentively to the serious young woman giving a cooing, gurgling account of the strange events that had befallen this masochistic son of the cruel Western god. It had reminded him of his own visit to Chieng Mai, in northern Thailand, where he had wandered equally helplessly from temple to temple, book in hand. Books tell no lies, and he had let the facts, dates, and architectural styles trickle deeply into his brain. But at the same time, he kept that penetrating sense of impotence because he could not *see* why one building was so much older than another, because he could not read the signs, and in the last instance, because he had not been born a Thai. The nuances that gave those things their flavor would remain hidden from him because, quite simply, they were not his. Even in the colonial cathedral of Lima, where he was more at home, he had decided to let it pass before his eyes like a brilliant decor, no more. You did not have a thousand lives. You had only one.

The voice by his side said that Raku IX was the adoptive son of Raku VII and a far greater potter than his brother Raku VIII, but Inni had stopped listening. He saw Riezenkamp showing out the Japanese and watching them go from behind the closed net curtains in the door. The little group walked as far as the bridge, gesticulating in the bright sunlight like a set of shadow puppets. Then one of the puppets turned around and became human again, walking back toward the shop. Riezenkamp quickly returned to his office and did not emerge until long after the bell had rung. The conversation was shorter this time.

The voice by Inni's side, which had just embarked on a discourse on the tea ceremony, halted, for the unmatched duo, art dealer and customer, giant and dwarf, were moving in the direction of the window where the bowl stood. Both had on their faces that expression Inni knew so well and which could mean only one thing: the two parties had come to an agreement about the same object, even though their intentions were totally different. Both would be receiving something—the Japanese the bowl, the dealer the money. Good breeding tempered any manifestation of the greed they were prey to. What followed next looked more like a sacred act than anything else. With a small key, Riezenkamp opened the display case as if it were a tabernacle. Something terrible is about to happen, though Inni. A bowl such as that will not allow itself to be removed with impunity. He noticed that the face of the man by his side had turned gray underneath the brown. The dark eyes followed the art dealer's large white hands closing around the bowl and lifting it out of the case. For a moment Inni thought the man was about to say something, but the wan, bloodless lips remained tightly closed in a face which itself looked like a Japanese mask. But what did it express? Hatred, certainly, but also weakness, caused by immense grief. Here was a man, thought Inni, who had long since lost the ability to feel grief over people and who had lodged all the grief he possessed in this black bowl.

The Japanese took it from the dealer. How much more did those hands belong to it! He put it down carefully, bent over it, and quickly and with a hissing noise sucked some air into his mouth and said something with long, deep throaty sounds. Only then was Inni able to see the bowl properly. A streak of lighter, rough dots ran through the deep darkness of its black interior like a gray Milky Way. Who would dare drink from it? The spotlight straight overhead was reflected in the bottom, but it seemed as if the bowl was reluctant to return the light that was so generously sent to it, and kept it greedily inside the deep black earth of which it was made. For the second time that day Inni thought of the earth in which he had buried the dove, and now something sinister had come into this light day, something sinister connected with the motionless man by his side, with the fixed gaze of the Japanese buyer, and with all those silent, closed objects around him.

"Well, Mr. Taads," said the art dealer, suddenly, "I am sorry, but there it is. The rules of the game. Still, you know as well as I do that there are more raku bowls." With a move of his hand he invited the Japanese into his office. The buyer picked up the bowl and followed him slowly and gravely.

"Taads," said Inni. "I once knew someone of that name. But he . . ." Inni checked himself. He couldn't very well say, "but he was a white man." This Taads gave him a long, silent look.

"I have no relations," he said finally. "I don't know any other Taadses. The only one I knew was my father, and he is dead. He once wrote a book, about mountains. I have never read it."

"Arnold Taads?"

"Yes, he was my father. Not that it meant much to him. Did you know him?"

"Yes."

"Did he ever mention me? My name is Philip."

"No, he never told me he had a son. I did know he had a wife."

"Had had, exactly. He tormented my mother into the grave. He left her when I was very young, and we never heard from him again. I gather he was a hard, egocentric man. He had brought my mother home from the Indies. I don't suppose he ever told you about that? He returned home with my mother and his parong. His parong he kept."

He turned away as if to indicate that as far as he was concerned, the subject was closed, and he peered at the empty space where the bowl had been.

"First they squandered them, and now they are taking them away again." He said it with bitterness, and for a moment the drawl had gone from his voice. "Let's get out of here."

"Did you want to buy that bowl?"

"Yes, but I haven't any money. I would need to save up for years for this bowl."

The new Taads who had come into his life walked out of the shop. Inni followed him. Now I am walking behind a Taads once again, he thought. Not until later did he remember that he had forgotten to say good-bye to the art dealer and had left his print behind. Transient life.

"Would you care for a drink?" he asked.

"I hate bars." And after a few moments, "Tell me, how did you know my father?"

"That is a long story."

"If you like, come and tell me about it at my home. I live in the Pijp. It's not far."

"Thank you."

They walked past the Rijksmuseum, which lay gleaming under its tall roofs like a treasure box of brick, and then alongside the swaying, shimmering water of the Ruysdaelkade. Ducks and gulls, quacking and squawking.

Philip Taads's universe was quite as idiosyncratic as that of his father. Nothing that led to it made you suspect where you would end up, and the contrast with the dilapidation that even in those years—as a forerunner of the disfigurement that was to afflict the whole city later—was eating its way through the nineteenth-century streets like a rapacious fungus, literally took your breath away. Behind the small man who, again like his father, looked neither up nor back, Inni threaded his way among the half-rotted wrecks of cars, evil-gleaming garbage bags, and double-parked delivery vans to a forlorn, peeling door behind which were steep, dark stairs whose top could not be seen from below. Inni felt as if he had set out on a pilgrimage, a penance that had everything to do with Arnold Taads and with his own past and not in any way with this thin, silent Easterner with his introspective monk's face.

The room they entered was very light and seemed at first sight completely empty. Everything in it was white. Here you were, far from the world, in a rarefied, cold mountain landscape, or rather in a monastery high in the mountains. At any rate, you were most certainly not in the Netherlands. Slowly Inni began to distinguish objects in the emptiness—a few white screens suspended from the ceiling and behind which nothing was visible, a low wooden bed, almost a plank, covered with a sheet and therefore more like a bier. It was clear that this Taads, too, lived on his own. There was not even a dog here to disturb the space and the silence. A faint smell of incense hung in the air. Philip Taads pointed to a cushion in the middle of the floor and sat down, in oriental posture, on a similar cushion opposite the first. Inni lowered himself uneasily and tried also to assume some sort of oriental pose, but ended up half-recumbent with one hand under his chin, a pashalike attitude which, as he was later to find to his satisfaction, the Enlightened One himself had assumed on occasion. This Taads also had a stern appearance, but Inni had grown too old to be intimidated by Taadses, dead or alive.

Fathers and sons. As Philip Taads did not speak but seemed to be rocking back and forth slightly to the rhythm of a repetitive interior prayer, Inni was able to give free rein to his thoughts. In one respect the son seemed to be unlike his father, for the striking of a clock brought no perceptible change in the situation. Time, then, played no role here. Inni asked himself what he was feeling at this moment. A kind of tedious distaste was the best way to describe it. There are things that ought not to be repeated, and this meditating Easterner ought not to have come drifting like a cloud in front of his father's memory. How strange, thought Inni, that memories are your only certainty. Anyone tampering with them is seen as an intruder. He was being forced to descend into the past, God knows, maybe to reconsider it. His aunt, Petra, the dog—all kinds of doors were being opened that would have been better left closed. What lay behind them had been properly filed, and that sufficed. One aspect of growing older is the refusal to admit new memories.

"My father despised me," said Philip Taads.

"He can hardly have known you."

"He did not want to know me. He couldn't bear the thought of leaving a trace behind him on earth. That I can understand, actually, but it was very unpleasant when I was a child. He never wanted to see me. He denied my existence. You were going to tell me how you knew him."

Inni told him.

"He looked after you better than he looked after me."

"It wasn't his own money. He didn't have to do anything for it."

"It sounds as if you liked him."

"I did."

Was this true? He had regarded Arnold Taads more as someone to whom such categories did not apply, as a natural phenomenon, as something that simply happens to be. It irritated him that he was now, in retrospect, forced to qualify his view. The present encounter was pointless. He had already had this experience before, or rather, someone else whom he had been very long ago had already had this experience and had told him about it. This Taads was crazy, too, and would come to a sad end, like his father.

"Have you spent much time in Asia?" Inni asked.

"Why?"

"It looks . . . Japanese here."

"I have never been to Japan. Modern Japan is vulgar. It was made diseased by us. It would destroy my dream to go there."

His dream. Goodness! This Taads was not afraid of big words. But perhaps *this* was a dream. The setting suggested it. The room that could not exist the moment you opened your eyes, the words that trickled slowly from the lips of this monkish man, the dark eyes that remained fixed on him as if to stop him from falling over.

Why did fathers make sons? With this son there were no curt, clipped sentences, no medals won by whizzing down snowy slopes, but rather the conversion of all that into slowness and emptiness. And yet, unmistakably, there was the same isolation, the same refusal.

"Shall I make tea?"

"Thank you."

When his host had vanished behind his screens like a silent shadow, Inni rose as if released, and walked, more or less on tiptoe, around the room, in which more and more objects loomed up. Or had these few books and picture postcards entered inaudibly and invisibly during the conversation, and had they, equally unheard and unseen, settled themselves on the floor against the baseboard? It was a riddle to him, as strange as the pictures on one of the cards: a raked area of powdery gravel in which, just slightly off center, three weathered stones of unequal size rested on an island of something that looked like moss. He remembered having seen such pictures before in books about Japan, but he had never seen a real one. Kneeling on the floor, he peered at the mysterious scene that, he did not know how, seemed to be reflected by this room, as if this bed, too, were not a thing you slept in but rather something akin to those stones, something that could express anything you cared to invest it with. Actually, thought Inni, this room, just like the gravel area with the three stones, would show to best advantage if there was nobody in it, not even the occupant, and no one to look at it. That area or garden or whatever you might call it could exist on its own, just like the universe, without inhabitants or spectators.

He shuddered and put the card back in its place, but this was not enough to release him from the room. The other cards represented real gardens with real shrubs, albeit trimmed into impossible euclidean shapes that were eerie in their perfection, and lawns that looked as if they had been licked smooth by a tongue, and blood-red sculptured autumn trees. Autumn! Here at least was a word that ought to evoke some idea of time. But time was precisely the element that was wholly absent from these photographs. A day's journey farther on, in another corner of the room, revealed a book with Japanese characters and the portrait of an old man on the cover. As he picked it up, his host returned.

"That is Kawabata," he said, "a Japanese writer."

"I see."

Inni studied the likeness of the old man. But was it an old man who was young or a young man who was old? From the uncommonly high forehead, silver-shiny hair swept back in a curve. The frail body was wrapped in dark, traditional dress. Leafing through the book from back to front, he saw the same man again, full length this time, receiving what must have been the Nobel Prize, because he stood facing the old king of Sweden, who raised his thin, applauding old man's hands especially high and far forward in the manner of well-bred northerners wishing to indicate that their enthusiasm is genuine. Because the author was photographed in profile here, you could see clearly how incredibly small and delicate he was. He stood bowed, wearing white socks and curious-looking sandals, and held the object he had just received firmly in his hands. Over a long, green robe he wore a black cloak down to the knees. Inni was not sure whether it was a kimono. Again it struck him how high the hair swept up from the small, inward-looking face. On the broad faces of the princes and princesses before him and, due to the height of the podium, also partly below him, lay an expression that could best be described as an anxious form of bewilderment.

Philip Taads had resumed his position on the floor, if *resumed* was the correct term for the strange way in which his body bent double and subsided in a silent, straight sliding movement. At the same time and without sound he put the lacquered tray with the two bowls of green tea on the rush mat. His host drank as Inni watched him through his eyelashes. Again the face was closed, but it was not the East that had drawn the curtains. He was faced here with someone who lived completely within himself. The idea of this man in this room seemed sinister. He wished he had not come.

They drank in silence.

"What do you do?" Inni asked finally, using the familiar form. When people are sitting face to face on floor cushions, there is no place for formality. Besides, they were the same age, he estimated.

"To earn money, you mean?" It sounded like a reproof.

"Yes."

"I work for a trading company. Foreign correspondence, three days a week. Letters in Spanish. They all think I am crazy, but they let me do as I like because I am good at it."

Spanish. Inni looked at his face but did not find what he was looking for. Javanese villagers had banished the memory of Arnold Taads, and this Philip had shorn his head like a monk, so that every contour of his face showed up twice as sharply. Someone who shaves his head takes away the modifying effect of the hair, so that nose, mouth, emotions, and everything else are exposed without mercy. But in the face of this Taads everything was under lock and key.

"Do you live alone?"

"Yes."

"And for the rest?"

"For the rest? Nothing. My part-time job pays enough to live on. And I live here."

"Are you always here?"

"Yes."

"Stabilitas loci."

"I don't understand."

"Stabilitas loci, that is one of the principles of the contemplative orders. Where you enter, you stay."

"Hm. Not a bad idea. What made you think of that?"

"There is something monastic about this place."

"And do you think that is ridiculous?"

"No." Only creepy, he thought, but he did not say so.

"Outside"—the word was uttered with scorn—"there is nothing for me."

"And here there is?"

"Myself."

Inni groaned inaudibly. The seventies. No sooner had they closed the door of the church behind them than they crawled like beggars to the bare feet of gurus and swamis. At last they were alone in a wonderful, empty universe that went zooming along on its homemade rails like a train without a driver, and they were shouting for help out of all the windows.

"I am preparing myself for something," said Philip Taads.

"For what?"

"For my deliverance." Not a moment's hesitation. "My dream. My deliverance." For the first time Inni asked himself whether the man opposite him was not simply stark staring mad. But the man looked as if it were perfectly natural for people to say such things, even though they had known each other for scarcely an hour, and maybe it was. He was, after all, a Taads, and Taadses used with the greatest ease—as Inni knew from experience—words that other people preferred to avoid. They lived one meter above the ground, at a level where those words had their natural domain. Perhaps they could even fly.

"Deliverance is a Catholic concept," said Inni.

"Not the way I mean it. The Catholics need someone else to deliver them. You can share in the deliverance. But that doesn't mean anything to me. I deliver myself."

"From what?"

"First of all from the world. That has proved easier than I thought. There's nothing to it. And then from myself."

"Why?"

"Life is a burden to me. It isn't necessary."

"Then you should commit suicide."

Taads did not reply for some time. Then he said softly, "I want to be rid of the thing I am."

"Thing?"

Inni took a sip of the tea, which had a deep, bitter taste. It was as if silence were being heaped up in the room.

"I detest the thing I am."

How long ago was it that Inni had heard this man's father say "I detest myself"? It was insufferable that a thought could travel from one man through a woman into another man. He wanted to get out of this room.

"I never talk about this with anyone," said Philip Taads. This was unmistakably a complaint, but the complainer was already out of the reach of any comforter. "Perhaps you'd rather I didn't bother you with it."

Such notions would never have occurred to Arnold Taads. So there was a difference after all.

"No," said Inni automatically. This was his first conversation with a thing, and he felt irreparably contaminated. He put down his bowl.

"I must go," he said.

The other did not reply but rose, again in one movement, the way a bamboo stem swishes up after being held down. He has got perfect control over the thing he is, at any rate, thought Inni, not without envy, as he laboriously got up from the floor.

"What I meant to say is that I find it unbearable to need a body in order to exist," said Taads.

A Catholic after all, thought Inni. The unclean body, an obstacle on the road to salvation; but before he could say anything, Philip Taads asked suddenly, "What kind of person was my father?"

Someone who killed himself, Inni was about to say, but was that really true? Arnold Taads had gone to his chosen destiny by an obscured, roundabout route. There was no need to saddle the son, who was already burdened with an inheritance, with this knowledge. A surfeit and a lack of father. Psychology, yuck.

"He was an uncompromising man who went his own way. I think he was very lonely, but he would never have admitted it. He did a lot for me, but not out of altruism. He did not like people, or so he said."

"Then we have at least something in common," said Philip Taads. He sounded pleased.

They walked toward the door together, but before they reached it, Philip Taads opened a cupboard in the wall that so far had seemed solid, and took a Penguin paperback out of it.

"By Kawabata," he said. "You need to read only the second story, 'Thousand Cranes.' When you've finished it, you can send it back, or if you like, you can return it to me yourself. I am always at home on weekends and on Mondays and Tuesdays."

The door closed soundlessly behind Inni. Now to take a big leap and soar away over those cavernous stairs to get out of this prison in which a man was tormenting himself, even though he called it deliverance!

Outside, the day had adapted itself to Inni's changed mood. A haze hung about the streets, giving the city an air of sadness. The passersby were still in summer dress, but the light, no longer transparent, draped their summery figures in an element of melancholy. As always when a natural phenomenon appeared to be getting the better of the normal course of events, Inni felt as though the city had no right to exist at all. This haziness had nothing to do with cars and houses but ought to have joined directly onto the grasslands of the polders. This thought gave rise to a feeling of anxiety, because it implied the dislocation of reality. He did not like being forced to notice how fragile everything was. This Taads was bound to keep preying on his mind. He had twice introduced the thought of death into this sunny day by what he said and by recalling the memory of his father from the formless past.

"The Wintrops refuse to suffer," Arnold Taads had said, but this had not been sufficient. The Wintrop that Inni himself was, refused not only to suffer but also to be confronted with the suffering of others. He had made his life one of constant movement, knowing from experience that this was the best way to escape from others when the need arose, and ultimately from himself, too.

He walked in the direction of the Vijzelstraat. From behind the

Mint Tower, which seemed to be rocking slightly in the heat that quivered in the shrouded sky, thunderclouds advanced like an army.

As he approached the Weteringplantsoen, he heard the sound of loud, rhythmic bells and whining, repetitive singing. A group of bald-pated members of the Hare Krishna sect came, in orange robes, bleating and bell-ringing across the pedestrian crossing. Swaying and with white, unshaven faces that refused to look at the bystanders, they were coming toward him. As always, he felt hate. People had no business to abandon themselves so shamelessly to a system. The thought he had had less than half an hour ago returned with renewed force: people were incapable of being alone in the world. No sooner had they buried the wretched god of the Jews and Christians than they had to go traipsing about the streets with red flags or in sloppy saffron sack dresses. Clearly, the Middle Ages would never end. He thought of Taads and how easy it was to imagine him, with his oriental face, walking among these people. But that was unfair. Philip Taads practiced his one-man religion—if it was that—alone in his homemade monastery. An anchorite in the desert of the Pijp. Inni remembered visiting the Benedictine monastery in Oosterhout with his friend the writer. The writer, never very talkative, had looked around for hours and finally asked one of the monks whether he had ever wanted to get out. The question had not surprised the old man in the least, and the reply came instantly. "The last time I felt that way was in 1929, when the heating didn't work."

They had laughed heartily at that, but then the monk had asked the writer: "And what about you? I don't suppose this is the first time you have visited a monastery? Have you never wanted to get in?"

His reply had been of an equally devastating simplicity, and Inni had always remembered it. "The world is my monastery," the writer had replied, and the monk had laughed in his turn and said he understood.

"The world is my monastery." But Taads had turned himself into a monk for the sole purpose, by his own account, of meditating himself to death. Surely that could not be based on any oriental doctrine. As soon as sacrifices were made, you were back at Golgotha, and clearly, Philip Taads could find no deliverance without slaughtering someone, even if it was himself.

"Nonsense, mere bravado," Inni muttered. "People who say they'll do it, won't." But even that seemed to be no longer true these days.

As though pulled by a string, he turned into a side street leading toward the Spiegelgracht. When he got there, he realized why. He had left his print at Riezenkamp's. For the second time that day, he entered the hallowed silence of the shop. None of the buddhas had stirred. Nothing and no one had disturbed their everlasting meditation.

"Aha, Mr. Wintrop," said the art dealer. "I was about to phone our friend Roozenboom, but now you are here yourself. I didn't know you knew Mr. Taads."

"I knew his father."

"Ah, did you." And after a moment's well-bred hesitation, "Someone from Indonesia?"

"No, from Twente."

"Ah, the mother, then. Hm, a strange man, a strange man. I have a standing agreement with him, that I will let him know whenever I have an important chawan."

"A chawan?"

"A tea bowl. Of a particular kind, that is. Only raku. No shino, no orige, even though you do get beautiful specimens among those, too. No, it has to be raku and nothing else, and preferably a Sonyu, that is, Raku VI. You know, the great masters, whether they are potters or kabuki actors, operate, if you can call it that, in dynasties."

"Mr. Taads gave me a lecture on it."

"Did he indeed. The difficulty is that the great bowls of these true masters are all known by name. Look"—he leafed through a book that was still lying in front of him—"there are still a few famous bowls by this Sonyu that have survived . . . komeki, the tortoise, that is black raku . . . and then you have kuruma, the cartwheel . . . a beauty, red raku . . . personally I like that one best . . . shigure, spring rain . . . also red . . . but all of them priceless, if they ever come up for sale at all. The only thing I can really hope for as far as Mr. Taads is concerned is a less well-known bowl by one of these gentlemen, but, well, the times are against him. The connoisseurs and the passionate collectors are being squeezed out by the investors. I offered him deferred terms, because I trust him implicitly. But he refused. 'That does not fit in with my plans.' So I imagine it will take some time. I shouldn't think he has a very high income, would you?"

"No idea. How did you get to know him?"

"Don't laugh. From yoga."

Yoga. It was difficult indeed to picture this tall, fleshy body in a yoga position.

"There was a rather curious ad in the paper, and both of us replied to it. Taads was already much into Zen at the time and knew much more about these things than I did. I was thinking more in purely plebeian terms—body exercise, relaxation, etcetera. No mumbo jumbo. But it took a grip on me. The teacher seemed to me, Dutch Calvinist that I am, quite as odd a customer as Taads—a South American Jew with a dash of Red Indian blood in him. A very compelling person."

It was as though Riezenkamp were having to suppress a slight shudder at this point. A shadow moved across his face and no doubt spread right down the white body underneath the worsted chalk-stripes.

"Yoga, proper yoga, should not be underestimated. This man, thank God, did not spin us any metaphysical yarn. He just sat there, a sort of latter-day saint, always dressed in black, and talked to us very slowly. He made us tighten and relax separate parts of the body and taught us how to forget them, not to feel them any more. Then they were simply no longer there. At first I thought it was wonderful. It gave me a tremendous feeling of well-being. But on Taads it had quite a different effect. After one of those sessions he had a terrible crying fit, as if he were about to throw up his whole inside, so violent. And another time he couldn't get his hands out of a cramp. Perhaps I ought not to tell you this, but it frightened the wits out of me. If that is the effect it has on him, I thought, what is it doing to me?

"Do you know, after a while you begin to realize that you cannot detach all these things from the rest of your life. If you were to go on with it, you would have to change your life, become a different person, if that were possible. I mean, you don't have to have a philosophy yourself or believe in anything, but it gradually alters your personality. At least that was how I felt about it. You change, you develop a different outlook on life—it isn't just a bit of gymnastics—well, and then, your outlook on life, on the world, that is, what you *are*. And this is very true in my case. Being an art dealer, a much-scorned species, I do, after all, have to function in the world. I began to wonder whether it wasn't going to do me more harm than good. I was quite used to myself as I was. For instance, I was beginning to find my glass of beer at Hoppe's rather vulgar, to mention something trivial. Let's put it this way: it called for more than I had, or than I was prepared to give, and in the end I stopped it." He rubbed his eyes briefly and continued. "I am surrounded by the sublime all day, even though I have a fairly perverse relationship with it. To put it bluntly, I hadn't the guts to go on. I explained it to the teacher and he understood. He told me he had twice given it up himself because he was afraid of losing himself. That was how he put it. He probably didn't mean the same thing as I did. Obviously, it's very far-reaching if you do that sort of thing professionally"—again that shudder—"but anyhow, he said he understood.

"Taads carried on with it. Whether he still does it now, I don't know. Maybe he has got just as far as the teacher by now. I never talk about it with him, out of embarrassment, I think. He seems to me the sort of person that goes to any lengths, and I think he has organized his entire life around it. And yet he still has that tenseness, that is what I find so strange. You never see him in a bar, women I have never heard him speak of, and the only time I have ever seen him talking to someone else was today, to you. And those bowls, of course, they have something to do with it as well. It is all connected with the tea ceremony and therefore with Zen. He lives in his own Japan, our friend. What do you think of it?"

"It doesn't really mean much to me," said Inni. "Strange wisdoms from the Far East being sold to the unhappy Western middle classes. But I daresay it's better than heroin."

Not much of an answer, he thought, but the subject did not interest him, or rather, he did not want to have anything to do with it.

"The curious thing is," said Riezenkamp, who evidently preferred to pursue his own line of thought, "that so much of what is being preached or claimed by those people—I still do take some kind of interest in it—is demonstrable nonsense, and this is true both for some theories on yoga and for the physical aspects of meditation, and that nevertheless the effect can prove beneficial."

"The same is true of the Last Rites," said Inni crustily, but of course, a Calvinist wouldn't understand about that. Riezenkamp was silent. Outside, a sudden rough gust of wind bent the branches of the trees with a furious blow. In a few moments it would be pouring rain, and he had no umbrella with him. This day was beginning to weigh heavily. A girl, dead doves, a shadow from the underworld, an oriental madman, sermons, and now this sudden decline of a summer day that disagreeably seemed to herald autumn, that sad season which should still be so far away.

The art dealer did not notice his impatience.

"I see Taads has given you his favorite book to read," he said. "I know it, it's superb. There is both a lot of action in it, and very little. It's full of nuances, small shifts with dramatic consequences. If anyone has ever succeeded in weaving the tea ceremony into a story, Kawabata has, brilliantly. You don't often find that, an object as the main character of a story."

To Inni's dismay he took yet another book out of the bookcase.

"I only show you this so you will know what shino looks like. If you have a physical image of it, you will understand the book better."

The white hands turned the pages. What exactly was so mysterious about bowls, or about chalices for that matter? Upside-down skulls that no longer contained anything, that were no longer turned toward the earth but toward heaven. They were things into which you could put something, but only something that came from above, from the higher world of suns, moons, gods, and stars. An object that could at the same time be empty and full was in itself somehow mysterious, but that could equally well be said of a plastic cup. So the material of which it was made must have something to do with it as well. The gold of the chalice evoked blood and wine. And when you looked at these shino bowls, it seemed inconceivable that anyone should ever drink anything from these gray and whitish chalices painted with light purple brush strokes, other than the rarefied, bitter green liquid Philip Taads had given him. If Christ had been born in China or Japan, tea would now be turned into blood every day on five continents. But in the tea ceremony it was not so much the tea that mattered, he realized, as the way in which you drank it. The form of the ceremony ultimately had to lead to an inner experience that pointed the way to the closed gardens of mysticism. What a strange animal was man, always somehow needing objects, "made" things with which to facilitate his journey to the twilit realms of the higher world.

Cars began to sound their horns outside. Somewhere a truck was blocking the road, and mankind, which not so long ago had landed on the moon in one graceful leap, uttered its displeasure with the enraged screams of an orangutan unable to find any bananas.

"In 1480," said Riezenkamp, "but nobody knows this, a witch cursed this spot and said that Amsterdam would perish in chaos and hellish noise."

He put his hand on the inscrutable buddha mask and said, "The falsification lies perhaps in this, that such faces, and all they ever uttered, could only come into existence in a world without noise." He paused briefly so as to allow the swelling wail of dozens of horns to be heard in its fullness, and continued. "Can you imagine how incredibly quiet it was everywhere, when the gentlemen from this world"—he made a vague circular gesture toward the battalions of meditating Asians behind him—"were hatching and proclaiming their ideas? Anyone who now tries to follow these ideas in order to find the road back to what they were talking about, is faced with obstacles that would have driven an entire tribe of oriental ascetics into the ravine. The world from which they felt it so necessary to retreat would have seemed idyllic to us. We live in a vision of hell, and we have actually got used to it." He looked at his statues and continued, "We have become different people. We still look the same, but we have nothing in common with them any more. We are differently programmed. Anyone who now wants to become like them must acquire a big dose of madness first; otherwise he will no longer be able to bear the life of our world. We are not designed for their kind of life."

It began to rain at last, and hard, too. The drops exploded on the shiny roofs of the cars, which did not stop honking. A few forlorn cyclists, bent under the castigating, lashing rain, tried to weave their way among the roaring vehicles.

"Do you know," said Riezenkamp, "sometimes I think we deserve heaven simply by living in these times. Nothing is right any longer. It's about time they dropped that damn thing. Just imagine the wonderful silence that would follow."

That night, when Inni Wintrop dreamed for the first time of the second Taads, he also dreamed for the second time of the first Taads. It was not a pleasant experience. The Taadses were having a conversation together, the content of which ceased to have any meaning as soon as he woke up. It was the sight of them that was so unpleasant. Impatient hatred against languid hatred, a tedious and then suddenly biting dialogue between two corpses. For there was no doubt, both Taadses were somewhere where they could not be seen except by someone whose eyes were closed, a tossing and turning dreamer who wiped the sweat from his face, woke up, went to the open window, and looked out over the black silence of the canal. What the dreamer felt was fear.

From another open window came the sound of a clock striking four. Inni groped his way back to bed and switched on the light. Half-open on his pillow lay the book by Kawabata, a mortally dangerous web spun out of gossamer words in which people were trapped and tea bowls were in command—bowls that preserved and destroyed the spirits of their previous owners or, as in this story, were themselves destroyed.

Four o'clock. He did not know whether he would fall asleep again. It was too late for a sleeping pill, but the risk that the watchmen of the realm of the dead would let out Arnold and Philip Taads a second time that night was too great. Why had the dream been so frightening? No one had threatened him, and what was spoken he had been unable to understand. But perhaps that was precisely the reason: he had quite simply not existed. It was only then he remembered that Philip Taads was not dead at all, but alive. *If* he was still alive. Inni got up and dressed. The first grayness was beginning to creep up from the paving stones, brushing against the walls and pulling the shapes of houses and trees out of the all-embracing protection of the night. Where to? He decided to retrace the route he had taken the day before.

Nothing irreparable had happened. The city had kept each place intact. Where the first dove had hit the car, he stopped. The dove had shed no blood, and there was nothing to be seen. He walked where he had cycled. On the back of his imaginary bike sat the imaginary girl. It would be like this when you were really old—a city full of imaginary houses and women, rooms and girls. The bridge by the park was now an ordinary roadway. He walked over the second dove, which was no doubt fast asleep underneath his feet. The park gates were open. The damp smell of soil. He searched for the spot where they had buried the dove but could not find it. The earth was still wet from the rain. Among the many water-logged footsteps must be hers, too. And his. It was as if they had been drowned. He could not find her house either. The darkness had gone, but the light had not yet become daylight. It looked as if the city were dreaming—a gruesome nineteenth-century dream of rows of brick houses and blind windows with net curtains like shrouds. No girls lived in the rooms behind them, and he could not possibly have lain there on a bed the previous morning, with a stream of golden hair in his hands. Did any people live here at all? As he walked, he listened to his own loud, lonely footsteps, and because he was listening, he quickened his pace. The dusty shape of the third dove was still imprinted on Bender's window. The rain had failed to wash it away. So it must all have really happened.

Behind Bernard's display window a beige screen had been let down. The yellow craziness of a first tram broke the spell, but all the seats were empty. The driver sat in it like a dummy. In place of the raku bowl there was nothing, but he did not have to close his eyes to see it—black, gleaming, and threatening—a harbinger of death. When he rang Philip Taads's bell, the door opened at once.

* * *

"I sleep very little" said Philip Taads. He was sitting in the same place as yesterday and wore a plain blue kimono. "Sleeping is senseless. A peculiar form of absence that has no meaning. One of all the people you are is resting, the others remain awake. The fewer people you are, the better you sleep."

"If you don't sleep, what do you do?"

"I sit here."

Here. That could only be the particular spot where he was actually sitting now.

"But what do you do?"

Taads laughed.

"Yoga?"

"Yoga, Zen, Tao, meditation, kono-mama, they're all just words."

"Meditate? What about?"

"The question is wrong. I think about nothing."

"Then you might as well be asleep."

"When I sleep, I dream. I don't have any control over that."

"Dreams are necessary."

Taads shrugged his shoulders. "For whom? I find them irritating. All kinds of people appear in them that I haven't asked to see, and things happen that I don't want. And make no mistake, these events and these people may not be real, although I am not sure what that means exactly, but you see them with your real eyes while you are asleep. They have measured it. Your eyes keep moving back and forth and follow those nonexistent people closely. I find that irritating."

"I dreamt of your father last night," said Inni. "And of you."

"That I find irritating, too," said Taads. "I was here. I wasn't with you. What did you dream?"

"You were both dead, and you were having a hostile conversation with each other. I couldn't make out what you were saying."

Taads rocked slowly from side to side.

"When I say I think about nothing," he said finally, "I don't mean nothing*ness*. That is nonsense. Tao is eternal and spontaneous. It has no name. You cannot describe it. It is at the same time the beginning of everything and the way in which everything happens. It is not-anything."

Inni did not know what to answer. Suddenly, behind the slow figure in his white monastery, he saw Taads senior looming up on his skis, speeding down a snowy, fairly steep slope.

"The trouble is," said Philip Taads, "that in these things the thought is not contained in the words. Zen uses few words and many examples. To someone who is not familiar with it, it all seems nonsense. All mysticism is always nonsense. Even Christian mysticism, where it overlaps with Buddhism, as it does in Meister Eckhart. To Eckhart, God is both being and nonbeing. You see, nothingness is never far away. The hole, is what the Buddhists call it."

Taads now made the face of someone about to quote something, and said, "I say this: God must be very I, and I must be very God, so all-consumingly *one* that this he and this I are one *is* and are in this isness eternally working at one and the same thing. But as long as this he and this I, that is, God and the soul, are not one single here and one single now, the I cannot work with or be one with the he."

"Isness?"

"Isticheit."

"A nice word." Inni savored it once again. "Isness."

It was as if Taads suddenly took courage. "According to Chuang Tzu . . ."

"Chuang who?"

"Tzu, a Taoist. All things are in a constant state of self-transformation, each in its own way. In this everlasting change, they appear and disappear. What we call 'time' plays no role whatsoever. All things are equal."

Inni heard the father—"I am a colleague of all that exists." For people who had never talked to each other, the Taadses were in amazing agreement, but the idea that a train of thought could be hereditary was unpalatable. What might his own vanished father have transmitted to him?

"But what does this have to do with Eckhart's god?"

"God is a mere word, too."

"I see."

"Reality and unreality," Taads continued, "good and evil, life and death, love and hate, beauty and ugliness, all things that are opposite are basically one and the same."

Now he looks like Jesus in the temple, thought Inni. He knows it all. If everything was the same, you wouldn't need to bother about anything.

"But how can you live with that in practical terms?"

Taads did not answer. In a homespun universe of fifty square meters, there was perhaps no need for an answer. Inni felt an uncontrollable urge to get up, and did so. I haven't had enough sleep, he thought. When he stood behind Taads, now a blue-swathed, gently rocking dummy whose lower half had disappeared into the floor, he said, "I thought all those doctrines or whatever you call them were meant to achieve harmony somehow with everything that exists. That seemed to me to contradict what you said yesterday. Someone who opts out, that is not harmony."

The blue shape slumped slightly.

"What's the use of all this meditation?" Inni noticed how his own voice had the high-pitched, I-have-you-there tone of a prosecutor in an American television courtroom.

"May I try to explain?" The voice sounded meek now, but it was a long time before it spoke again.

"If you have never thought about it in this way, what I say must sound like nonsense. If you simply want to look at it in purely Western terms, I am a pathological case, right? Someone who for whatever reasons, background, circumstances, the whole lot, cannot cope any longer and says he has had enough of it. It happens that I am not the only one. What the East has given me is the thought that this I of mine is not so unique. Nothing much will be lost when it disappears. It isn't important. I am a hindrance to the world, and the world is a hindrance to me. There will only be harmony if I get rid of both at once. What dies in that case is a bundle of circumstances that bore my name, plus the limited and moreover constantly changing knowledge that these circumstances had about themselves. It doesn't matter to me. I have learnt not to be afraid. That in itself is quite a lot, and I am not capable of anything more. In a Zen monastery I would probably get the stick mercilessly, because it's all no good, but it satisfies me. What I have achieved is negative. I am no longer afraid, and I can quietly dissolve myself the way you dissolve a bottle of poison in an ocean. The ocean won't feel any ill effect, and the poison has been freed from a great burden; it does not have to be poison any more."

"And is that the only solution?"

"What I lack is love."

The words were uttered so desolately that for a moment Inni felt an impulse to lay his hand on that stubbornly self-absorbed head. He thought of a line from a Spanish or South American poet he had once read somewhere, which he had never been able to forget: "Man is a sad mammal that combs its hair."

"Would you please sit down again?" The voice sounded now more drawling than ever and had an undertone of protest. Inni felt he was disturbing an established order here—here, too. He looked at his watch.

"You can't stand any more of it, can you," said Taads.

"There's an auction at Mak van Waay's." It sounded ridiculous.

"There's plenty of time. You want to get away."

"Yes."

"You think I'm crazy."

"No, I don't. But it oppresses me."

"Me, too. But what is it exactly that oppresses you?"

Inni said nothing and went to the door. When he reached it, he turned. Taads had closed his eyes and was sitting very still.

If this were a movie, I would have walked out long ago, thought Inni. He saw himself standing by the door, tired, balding, a man of the world in decline, someone on his way to an art auction, someone who had strayed into the house of a madman.

"I could have forced myself to adapt," said Taads. "In this world the individual self is of such importance that it is allowed to become absorbed in itself and to grub around in its trivial personal history for years on end with the help of a psychiatrist, so as to be able to cope. But I don't think that is important enough. And then suicide is no longer a disgrace. If I had done it earlier, I would have done it in hatred, but that is no longer the case."

"Hatred?"

"I used to hate the world. People, smells, dogs, feet, telephones, newspapers, voices—everything filled me with the greatest disgust. I have always been afraid I might murder somebody. Suicide is when you have been all around the world with your fear and your aggression and you end up by yourself again."

"It remains aggression."

"Not necessarily."

"What are you waiting for then?"

"For the right moment. The time has not yet come." He said it amiably, as if he were talking to a child.

"You are crazy," said Inni impotently.

"And that is also a mere word." Taads laughed and started rocking from side to side, a blue, human pendulum counting down the time to an as yet invisible moment when the clockface would be allowed to melt and float away to a realm where no numbers existed. He was no longer looking at Inni and seemed almost happy, an artist after the performance. The audience slowly opened the door. Street sounds, which did not belong to this room, entered, but Taads did not look up. The door closed behind Inni with a sucking noise, as if as much air as possible were trying to escape with him to the outside world where the anarchic freedom of the Amsterdam day enveloped him. He needed a shower before going to the auction. He would not visit this Taads again for some time.

Whether his Catholic past had anything to do with it, Inni did not know, but it turned out otherwise. From time to time he made what he called a pilgrimage to the monastery high up in the mountains. It gave him a pleasant feeling of continuity. Taads was always at home and there was no further talk of suicide, so that Inni began to suspect that the lonely monk had decided to allow the moment of his chosen and his natural death to coincide. The seventies rolled unhurriedly through time, and the world, like Inni himself and the city in which he lived, seemed slowly to disintegrate. People lived alone, and in the evenings they flocked despairingly together in brown, crowded cafés. The women's weeklies told him that he had reached the male menopause, and this fitted in amazingly well with the collapse of the stock exchange and the torn-up streets of Amsterdam, which by way of compensation, shifted its position agreeably farther and farther into Africa and Asia. He still lived on his own, traveled widely, and fell in love from time to time, though he found it extremely difficult to take this seriously. For the rest, he did what he had always done. As far as he could see, the world was moving, in an orderly capitalist fashion, toward a logical, perhaps provisional, perhaps permanent, end. When the dollar fell, gold rose; when interest rates went up, the property market collapsed; and as the number of bankruptcies multiplied, rare books increased in value. There was order in this chaos, and anyone who kept his eyes open was in no danger of crashing into a tree, though admittedly you needed a car.

After the bald-headed bell ringers, there now appeared tall white turbans, rastafari hairdos, and Jesus children in the streets. The end of time was at hand, and he did not think that was a bad thing. The deluge should not come after us; we ought to experience it. A Renaissance drawing, a Cerutti suit, his own worries, a Gesualdo madrigal, against this background acquired a relief that calmer times would not have accorded them; and the prospect of presently seeing politicians, economists, and nations sinking into a gigantic muck heap of their own making gave him tremendous satisfaction. His friends explained to him that this was a frivolous attitude, both nihilistic and wicked. He knew it was not, but did not contradict them. He thought that, unlike most people, he had simply refused to let himself be brainwashed by newspapers, television, eschatologies, and philosophies into believing that "in spite of everything" this was an acceptable world simply because it existed. It would never become acceptable. Beloved maybe, acceptable never. It had been in existence for only a few thousand years, something had gone irrevocably wrong, and now a fresh start had to be made. The loyalty to objects, to people, or to himself, which he felt in his everyday life, altered nothing in this insight. The universe could do quite well without this world, and the world could do quite well without people, things, and Inni Wintrop for a while. But unlike Arnold and Philip Taads, he did not mind waiting for events to take their course. After all, it might take another thousand years. He had a first-class seat in the auditorium, and the play was by turns horrific, lyrical, comic, tender, cruel, and obscene.

Five years after his first encounter with Philip Taads, Inni received a phone call from Riezenkamp. They, too, had met several times during these five years, and Taads had often been the subject of their conversation.

"Mr. Wintrop," said Riezenkamp's voice in the telephone, "I think the moment has arrived. I picked up something quite remarkable for our friend Taads at the Drouot auction, though I admit I can't quite imagine how he will be able to pay for it. He is coming to have a look at it. Would you like to be there?"

"A chawan?" asked Inni. He had done his homework.

"Classical akaraku. A marvel."

The eternal repetition of events. As he crossed the bridge over the Prinsengracht and the Spiegelgracht, he could already see Taads, a solitary figure in the rain. A great sadness descended on him, and he made up his mind not to show it. Somehow or other they had reached the last phase of this crazy affair.

The autumn wind chased tatters of orange and brown leaves across the pavement toward Taads, so that it looked as though, in spite of the rain, he was standing in a flickering, moving fire. But rain or fire, it could not hurt him. He stood nailed to the ground, his gaze fixed on the bowl in the window. Inni joined him but said nothing. The bowl had the same color as the dead leaves, all dead leaves together—the gleam of candied ginger, sweet and bitter, hard and soft, the luxurious fire of decay. It was a wide bowl, almost clumsy, not made by man but born in an unnameable prehistory. Whereas the black bowl had been threatening, this one was beyond such interpretations. The thought that things had to be seen by people in order to exist was not valid here, for if there were such a thing as a nirvana for objects, this raku tea bowl had reached it aeons ago. Inni realized that Taads dared not go into the shop. He looked at his face sideways. It was more oriental, more closed than ever, but in the eyes burned a fire that inspired terror. When Inni turned away he saw Riezenkamp inside the shop gazing at Taads as Taads was gazing at the bowl. As in old drawings explaining the rules of perspective, he could have drawn the line that ran from himself to Riezenkamp, from Riezenkamp to Taads, from Taads to the bowl.

Someone had to break the spell. Gently he touched Philip Taads's arm.

"Come on, let's go inside," he said.

Taads did not look up but allowed himself to be escorted in.

"Well, Mr. Taads," said Riezenkamp. "I did not exaggerate, did I?"

"I should like to hold it."

The art dealer's large body bent over toward the display case, and with an infinitely careful movement he lifted the bowl out.

"Here we are. I'll put it down on this table. The light is best here."

When the bowl stood on the table, Taads came a step closer. Inni waited for him to take it into his hands, but that moment was still a long way off. He stared, muttered something, and walked around the table so that the others had to move aside. He looked, Inni thought, at the same time like a hunter and a hunted animal. At last his hand reached out. One finger moved very lightly over the surface and then, again slowly, as though it were sacrilege, slid inside the bowl. No one spoke. Then Philip Taads suddenly picked up the bowl with both hands and raised it high as if in consecration. He brought the base close to his eyes and opened his mouth as if to say something, but remained silent. Gently he put the bowl down again.

"Well?" asked Riezenkamp.

"Raku IX, I think."

"Why?"

"Because it is fairly light," said Taads. "But of course I am not telling you anything new. It is not one of his masterpieces, for as far as I know those are all black. And the stamp is round, so maybe it is one of the two hundred chawan he made on the death of the first Raku, Chojiro."

He looked at Riezenkamp, who nodded imperceptibly.

"Chojiro," Taads continued, but now addressing himself more to Inni, "learnt his art from Rikyu, the greatest tea master of all times. Look, here, the color of a bowl was intended to bring out that strange green of Japanese tea. And there are also rules about the shape, all of which were drawn up by Rikyu, how the bowl should feel when you hold it, its balance, the way it feels to the lips"—he lifted it briefly to his mouth like someone trying on a pair of shoes—"and of course the temperature. The tea must not feel too hot or too cold to your hand when you hold it, but exactly as you would like to drink it. Have I passed the exam?" he suddenly added.

"Everything you say about its origins I have here," said Riezenkamp, waving an envelope. "You ought to set up as an art dealer. You are better qualified than I."

Taads did not answer. He closed his slender hands around the bowl.

"I want it," he said.

Inni realized that money would now have to be discussed, and he turned away. Taads and Riezenkamp disappeared into the little office. It did not take long. When they reemerged, Taads's face wore an empty, lost expression. He has got what he wants, thought Inni, who knew from experience that this is not always pleasant. Taads started wrapping the bowl in very thin paper he had brought out of the office. He did not speak.

"I've chilled a bottle of champagne for this memorable occasion, Mr. Taads," said Riezenkamp.

"That is most kind of you, Mr. Riezenkamp, but I am afraid it would be wasted on me. It would give me great pleasure, though, if you two drank it together. I will send you an invitation soon to come and drink from this bowl. I hope you will both come." He solemnly shook hands with them, even making something of a bow, and left.

From the window they watched him go, an Indonesian walking down the street with a box.

"There he goes with his baby," said Riezenkamp. "Do you know, it does not make me feel at all happy. For years he has been coming here, and now that it has happened, so quickly, so dryly really, I don't like it. I suppose it is my upbringing, but I feel just like Judas."

"Judas?"

"Forget it, it's stupid nonsense. But I shall miss him."

"I expect he'll drop in from time to time."

"No, I don't think he will. There was just one thing he wanted all these years, and now he has got it. Now he has nothing more to want. Not from me at any rate."

"Talking of Judas . . . what did that bowl cost?"

"A figure with four noughts. He must have saved up for it all his life, as a manner of speaking. And he actually had it in cash!"

"The exact amount? But he hadn't seen the bowl yet, had he?"

"I don't know if he had any more on him, but he paid what I asked for."

Four noughts, reflected Inni. That could be anything from ten thousand to ninety thousand. But if Riezenkamp did not want to tell him, he was not going to ask. There was sure to be someone who knew what that bowl had fetched at Drouot's, and the rest was easy to calculate. That then was the Judas element.

"I wouldn't say no to a glass of champagne," he said.

"I wonder," said Riezenkamp when he had poured out the first glass, "when he will invite us to a tea ceremony. Have you ever been to one?"

Inni shook his head.

"It is not very difficult," said the art dealer, "as long as you remember what it means to the Japanese. Of course, it is highly ritualized."

"And very tiring. You have to sit on your knees the whole time, don't you?"

"There comes a moment when you don't feel that anymore. But of course it is ridiculous for a Westerner to do it. For that reason I hope this cup, or rather this bowl, will pass us by. Because you can be sure he has got it all worked out exactly, our solitary friend."

Inni was thinking of Taads, who had now retreated to his mountain with his bowl, and he tried to think something connected with this, but he did not know what.

* * *

The invitation came a few weeks later. A brief note informed Inni and Riezenkamp that they were invited and that, unless he heard to the contrary, Taads would expect them one Saturday in November, a dreadful day of storm and hail, as it turned out. But even Nature herself seemed to have no power over Philip Taads's domain, for the silence in his attic more than compensated for the tugging of the wind at the windows. A change had taken place in the room. Subtle shifts had occurred which, if you looked carefully, had made the space asymmetrical. The kakemono with the flowers had gone, but instead of the painted ones there were now real flowers, one dark-purple and one gold-colored chrysanthemum, the colors of Advent and autumn. The book with the portrait of Kawabata had gone, too. The area where the ceremony was to take place was not in the center of the room but somewhere to the right, in a corner where a bronze kettle of water was steaming over a small spirit stove. Where the kakemono had been, there now hung a smaller scroll with calligraphic characters. They reminded Inni of a fast skier, drawn in mid-movement as he came down a snow-clad slope at full speed.

Taads, who had left the door ajar, was still behind his screens. Riezenkamp took a close look at the calligraphy and then knelt down on the mat in front of a primus stove, on one of two minuscule cushions that had been put ready there. He beckoned to Inni to do likewise.

"This is not going to be funny," said Inni. "How long are we supposed to sit like this?"

But the art dealer gave no reply. He had closed his eyes. Oh, if anyone could have seen them now! Riezenkamp was wearing a suit of anthracite-colored flannel. His large hands lay spread out flat on his thighs, causing his cuffs to stick out. These were fastened with two fairly large gold art nouveau cuff links in which the deep blue glow of lapis lazuli was caught. The same color recurred in his silk tie and contrasted almost savagely with the pale pink of his shirt. Jermyn Street, Inni estimated. And shoes from Agee's. There were lots of auctions in London, that was a fact. He himself had taken the precaution of wearing fairly loose corduroy trousers with a beige cashmere turtleneck pullover from the Burlington Arcade. Two Englishmen in Japan, waiting for things to come. Kneeling! How often had he done that before? On hard benches, on cold freestone altar steps, on marble, on gold cushions, in front of his bed in his boarding school dormitory, in the dark hole of a confessional, for punishment in a corner of the refectory while all the others were eating, before the Holy Virgin, before the Sacred Heart, before the Most Sacred Sacrament, by baptismal fonts, and by coffins, always in that same doubled-up posture, that unnatural fold in the body which was supposed to express humility and respect. He looked around the room. Where else could this be seen, two middle-aged men kneeling together by a burning flame in an Amsterdam attic beleaguered by the winter wind?

Taads entered, or rather, he emerged from behind one of his shadowy screens. He was wearing a short kimono today—a bit like the one the Nobel Prize winner had worn in the vanished book—over a long rust-colored robe, chasuble over alb. He was carrying a jug that turned out to contain water. He made a small bow, and they bowed back. He disappeared and reappeared, this time carrying a tall, round, black-lacquered box. Fine gold threads shimmered through the glossy black. Then there came, in succession, a tray of small biscuits; the autumn-fiery raku bowl; a long, narrow wooden object, very soberly cut out of bamboo with a small curvature as though of a very long finger, only the tip was bent; a kind of shaving brush made of open-worked, exceedingly fine reed or bamboo; and finally a broad, somewhat rustic bowl and a wooden cup with a long handle. Taads placed all these things around him, doubtlessly in predetermined positions. All his movements were like those of a slow dancer, and very precise. The silence remained near total—a rustling of cloth, the hiss of boiling water, the blowing of the wind. Yet the silence was so all-powerful that it seemed as though these objects, of whose function Inni was ignorant, took an active part in it and were themselves deliberately silent while at the same time expressing, by means of their perfect forms, that it was an intentional silence. Inni looked at Riezenkamp, but he made no response. He sat perfectly motionless, his eyes fixed on Taads's lean, slow-moving figure opposite.

With a silk napkin Philip Taads lightly wiped first the bamboo stick, which was hollow at its curved end, and then the long-handled cup. He shifted the lid slightly from the heavy bronze kettle, scooped out some water which he put into the raku bowl in which he then washed the bamboo brush, or whisk, or whatever it was. Then he slowly poured the water into the wide, rougher bowl and wiped the raku bowl with a simple cotton cloth. Inni noticed that he picked up, turned, and put back each object in a special way, but how and why he was unable to say, because despite the slowness of the movements, it all seemed to be done very quickly, as if it were one, long flowing action, a long, curving course of ritual obstacles whereby the hands sometimes assumed positions like those in a Balinese dance, or at any rate like different, non-European hands. Twice the long, thin stick was dipped inside the lacquered box. Inni saw a shadow of green tea powder rain down into the ginger fire of the raku bowl. Then Taads poured boiling water from the deep wooden spoon into the bowl, once, and stirred the mixture with rapid, brusque whisks of the brush. Perhaps you should not call it stirring, since it was more of a soft and yet vehement beating. In the bottom of the bowl, which now seemed to be verging toward red, a frothy pale green lake appeared. For a moment all movement stopped. More silent than it was now, it could not become. And yet it seemed as though the silence grew more dense and they were being immersed in an element of a more dangerous, more solid intensity.

Then, with a strange flick of his right hand, Taads rotated the bowl slightly while it rested in his left hand, pushed it toward Riezenkamp, and bowed. Riezenkamp bowed also. Inni held his breath. Riezenkamp then rotated the bowl twice (Twice? More times? He would never know, any more than he would be able to disentangle the threads of this whole knot of pregnant actions), lifted it to his mouth, drank twice, then a third time, while making a slight slurping sound. He then examined the bowl attentively from all sides, without holding it too high, turned it while it rested in his left hand, again with that strange circular flick, back to an existing or imaginary position, and pushed it across the mat to the host.

How often, thought Inni, had he poured the cruet of water into a golden chalice, whereupon the priest, with a quick twist of the hand, would let the blood, diluted with water, swirl around for a moment and would then drain the chalice in one flowing, sucking draught? It was the same here at this last supper. Fresh water from the kettle, the bowl was rinsed, the same actions, the same bow, and now it was Inni who held the flaming, fragile shape in his hands. He drank with closed eyes, and again, until at the third sip he opened his eyes and sucked the last green drops out of that dusky red, closed abyss. *Do this in remembrance of me*. Like Riezenkamp, he examined the bowl from all sides as if trying to burn its shape forever into the soul. He rotated it in what he thought was the right direction and pushed it back to Taads, almost hurriedly, as if that would avert the danger. As he did so, he saw that Taads's eyes were fixed on him, but whether they saw him he could not tell. The whole face shone with an unapproachable rapture, as if this Taads was in an even remoter and stranger place than that in which his guests were kneeling.

They bowed. Taads stood up, as usual in one long drawn-out movement, and took away the spoon, the lid of the kettle, and the rinsing bowl. He returned to fetch the lacquered box and the bowl, and finally the water. Riezenkamp also rose, and Inni followed suit, with some difficulty because of pins and needles in his feet. He suddenly felt dizzy. Taads came toward them and, as it were, forced them in the direction of the door.

"Thank you, Mr. Taads, that was most remarkable," said Riezenkamp. Taads bowed but did not reply. A smile had appeared on his face, strange and distant, seeming to accentuate the oriental in his face. He can no longer speak Dutch, thought Inni. Or he doesn't want to. No one spoke another word. Taads bowed once more, a farewell. They bowed back. The door closed behind them, softly and decisively.

In silence, like two thieves after a major burglary, the two men descended the endless stairs. Outside, the wind was waiting for them with a blow of hail on the jaw. Mouths closed, they walked through the storm to Riezenkamp's shop. The art dealer left the CLOSED sign hanging in the door, drew the curtains, and poured out two large malt whiskeys—smoke and hazelnut.

"Sometime," he said, and his voice sounded as tired as Inni felt, "I will tell you all about the tea ceremony. All those things have a history and a meaning of their own. You can study them for years." He made a vague gesture to a cupboard behind him in which rows of books shimmered behind glass.

Inni shook his head. "Not just now, thank you. I have seen enough of it for a while."

They drank. Outside, the gale whined in the bare branches, and the hail beat holes in the tomb-black water of the canal.

"That was a requiem mass for three men," said Inni.

Riezenkamp looked up and said, "Perhaps I ought not to have sold him that bowl."

"Nonsense." Inni shrugged his shoulders. An immense sadness had come over him. Because of the two Taadses, because of fate, which goes its own way, because of the lost years, and because of the impossibility of the world. He looked at his watch. Half past two.

"I'll go and see what the market has been up to today," he said.

Riezenkamp laughed. "I can tell you that with my eyes shut," and his hand made a slow, downward-sliding movement. "Sauve qui peut," he said.

Sauve my hat, thought Inni, and said good-bye.

In the days that followed, Inni felt an inclination at times to go and visit Taads, but their leave-taking had been too final for that. Three weeks later he received a phone call, and rang Riezenkamp at once.

"I've just had a call from Taads's landlady. She said she had not seen him for several days, but that was not unusual because he always did creep in and out—those were her words."

"Well?"

"But now she has received a letter from him saying she should phone me."

"To tell you what?"

"It didn't say anything else. She was to phone me. She asked me if I would come."

"To do what?"

I'll give you three guesses, thought Inni, but he did not say it. He heard a deep sigh at the other end of the line.

"Are you going?" asked Riezenkamp.

"Yes, I am setting off now. Are you coming?"

"Of course." Clever, how someone could express the self-assurance of a whole class in two syllables.

They met outside Taads's door and rang the landlady's bell. She gave Riezenkamp the key.

"I'm not going up," she said, "I don't trust it a bit."

If Riezenkamp felt anything at all, he did not show it. He turned the key resolutely in the lock and opened the door. The room was empty, the screens had been rolled up, there was no one to be seen. But in the middle of the floor, broken into a hundred pieces, there lay what could only be the raku bowl, smashed with great force.

On the gleaming, gold-colored mat the fragments lay scattered like bits of congealed and withered blood.

"We shall find nothing more here," said Riezenkamp, and closed the door softly.

A few days after they had reported the disappearance of Philip Taads, they were called by the police in IJmuiden to identify a body that answered the description they had given. For a moment they gazed in silence at the blue monster on the white sheet. They said, yes, that is Philip Taads.

This time it was not a frozen but a drowned man who was cremated. Bernard Roozenboom had gone with Inni and Riezenkamp, although no one quite knew why.

"Let's say that I was responsible, in part at least, by sending you to Riezenkamp. If I understood it properly, our tea-ist would have done this anyway, but at least you wouldn't have had anything to do with it."

The cremation took place in a dismal neighborhood on the outskirts of Amsterdam, where none of the three men had ever been before. Bernard's Rover drove through drab, empty suburbs full of hospitals and factories.

"Not exactly the road to paradise," Bernard said.

They were the only mourners. The coffin stood under a gray cloth on a platform with four bouquets of flowers, one of them from Taads's office—asters.

"There's no minyan," muttered Bernard, and suddenly Inni remembered the only time he had seen Bernard Roozenboom downcast. That had been in Florence, years ago. They had lunched copiously at Doney's and were walking around the city at random. Suddenly they found themselves standing in front of an imposing, not very large building. "Well I never," Bernard had said, "if it isn't the synagogue," and they had gone inside. After the brilliance of the Florentine churches, its interior was of a welcome sobriety. There was one man inside, gazing forward in total silence. At exactly five o'clock, when the clock of a nearby church struck the hour, a man in full pontificals entered and sat down. "Oh, god," Inni heard Bernard say, "it is Sabbath and there is no minyan." And when Inni looked at him questioningly, he continued, "If there aren't ten adult men present, the gazzan cannot begin." It remained silent. "How long will they sit here like that?" asked Inni. "One hour," came the answer. During that hour it was as if he could see Bernard growing smaller. Two tourists entered, but left again in fright. After an hour the gazzan rose and left, and they too went outside. Bernard had never mentioned the incident since, nor had Inni, but that was because he did not know what to say.

A man in a black suit came up to Riezenkamp and asked him something. Riezenkamp shook his head, no, no one wished to speak. With a click, a tape recorder started the Air from the Third Suite by Bach. The coffin had slid out of sight even before it was finished. The whole ceremony, if you could call it that, lasted five minutes. Then the world had settled its accounts with Philip Taads. When they came out into the open air, the dead man descended in the form of gray, damp snow on the shoulders of their overcoats. The only thing missing was a dove.

That night Inni dreamed of the two Taadses. The first one frozen, the second drowned—that was how they appeared at his bedroom window in a mood of mad, barbaric mirth, arms flung around each other, shouting inaudibly. Inni got out of bed and went to the window, behind which there was nothing to be seen but the swaying of skeletal branches coated with a glaze of ice. So there clearly existed two worlds, one in which the Taadses were, another in which they were not, and Inni was glad to be still in the latter.

On the day destined for his self-immolation, Rikyu invites his chief disciples to a last tea ceremony. One by one they advance and take their places. In the tokonoma hangs a kakemono, a wonderful writing by an ancient monk dealing with the evanescence of all earthly things. The singing kettle, as it boils over the brazier, sounds like some cicada pouring forth his woes to departing summer. Soon the host enters the room. Each in turn is served with tea, and each in turn silently drains his cup. According to established etiquette, the chief guest now asks permission to examine the tea equipage. Rikyu places the various articles before them with the kakemono. After all have expressed admiration of their beauty, Rikyu presents each of them to the assembled company as a souvenir. The bowl alone he keeps. "Never again shall this cup, polluted by the lips of misfortune, be used by man." He speaks, and breaks the vessel into fragments.

Okakuro Kakuzo
The Book of Tea